Metaphorosis

April 2018

Beautifully made speculative fiction

Also from Metaphorosis Books

Reading 5X5: Readers' Edition
Reading 5X5: Writers' Edition

Best Vegan Science Fiction & Fantasy

Best Vegan SFF of 2017
Best Vegan SFF of 2016

Metaphorosis Magazine

Metaphorosis: Best of 2017
Metaphorosis: Best of 2016
Metaphorosis 2017: The Complete stories
Metaphorosis 2016: Nearly Complete Stories
Monthly issues

by B. Morris Allen

Susurrus
Allenthology: Volume I
Tocsin: and other stories
Start with Stones: collected stories
Metaphorosis: a collection of stories

Metaphorosis

April 2018

edited by
B. Morris Allen

Metaphorosis Books

Neskowin

ISSN: 2573-136X (online)
ISBN: 978-1-64076-106-3 (e-book)
ISBN: 978-1-64076-107-0(paperback)

April 2018

Copyright

Metaphorosis Publishing

Metaphorosis offers beautifully written science fiction and fantasy. Our projects include:

Metaphorosis Magazine

Metaphorosis, a weekly magazine of SFF short stories, including stories from all the authors in this anthology. Find out more at magazine.metaphorosis.com, and sign up to be notified of new stories.

Metaphorosis Books

Recent books from Metaphorosis can be found at <u>books.metaphorosis.com</u>, and include:

Metaphorosis 2017

Metaphorosis 2016

All the stories from *Metaphorosis* magazine's second year.

Almost all the stories from *Metaphorosis* magazine's first year.

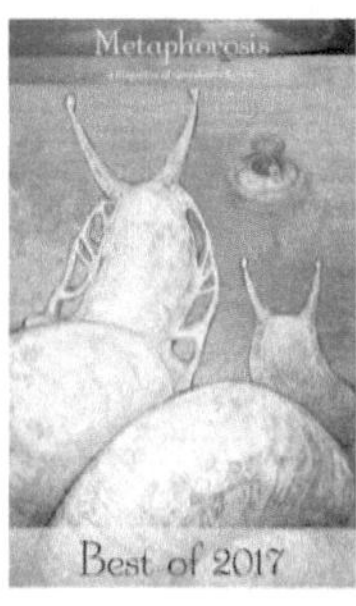

Metaphorosis:
Best of 2017

The best science fiction and fantasy stories from *Metaphorosis'* 2nd year.

Metaphorosis:
Best of 2016

The best science fiction and fantasy stories from *Metaphorosis'* 1st year.

Reading 5X5	**Reading 5X5**
Five stories, five times	*Writers' Edition*
Twenty-five SFF authors, five base stories, five versions of each – see how different writers take on the same material.	All the stories from the regular, readers' edition, plus two extra stories, the story seed, and authors' notes.

Best Vegan SFF of 2017

The best vegan science fiction and fantasy stories of 2017!

Best Vegan SFF of 2016

The best vegan science fiction and fantasy stories of 2016!

Susurrus

A darkly romantic story of magic, love, and suffering.

Bye Bye Skinny Cow

Hamilton Perez

"Excuse me," Cash tried again, "you're not a doctor, are you?" Another bemused look and shake of the head. "Oh, okay, thanks anyway," he said to their backs. The warm bundle in his arms groaned uncomfortably. It was the first Cash had heard from him all day. He took it as a good sign—beggars not choosers and all.

One after the other, people came and went from the office, filtering in and out fluidly by some alien osmosis that always kept Cash at bay. Sure, he could enter. But if he entered uninvited, he might be asked to leave, and then there would be no hope for him.

Cash watched them lead their sick or injured, augmented or gene-spliced companions beside them: furry lizards in need of hormones, bipedal hamsters overdue for flu shots, half-cat half-dog—*cags*—to be spayed or neutered. Unnatural creatures born from science and an excess of money. They all looked at Cash and his raw need with perplexed annoyance.

Are you a doctor? Excuse me, are you a doctor? You're not a doctor, are you? Hey, I'm not asking for money or anything, but are you a doctor?

"I don't carry cash," someone said in passing.

It felt prophetic.

"Young man..." a voice called, "I don't know if you should be out here doing that." An old woman stood behind him, round as Granny Smith apples and just as sour. She was leaving the office with a disgruntled Pekingese in matching attire, and gave Cash a dubious look in passing. "You know there's a shelter just down the street," she said like an accusation.

"Thank you," was all Cash could manage. He didn't want any trouble. He just wanted her to go. Instead she stood there, and Cash felt the weight of her eyes scrub him down from his mop of blond hair to dark-stained pants that quit before his ankles. She sneered at the knobby head of the guitar peeking over his shoulder, and when her eyes fell on the black and white Jack Russell cradled in his arms, she scrunched her face in disapproval. "*Thank you*," Cash said again to appease her.

Ultimately, the woman merely shook her head and slumped into her car before heading home disgruntled, though Cash felt the itch of her eyes linger on his skin for some time after.

The sun was beginning to set. Business hours were almost up. This was the third office he'd been to today. The others had told him they couldn't help without an appointment. The technician at the last office offered dog treats as a consolation. "He's not eatin..." Cash said on his way out the door.

Now the sky above him reddened and bruised, begged for the cold relief of night. An imminent despair tapped at his back, though still he shook it off. *No... Not yet*, he told it, and occasionally wondered if he'd spoken aloud.

It was almost an hour before a determined looking man in a white button-down and blue tie stepped from the office. His clothes were crisp and perfectly pressed, his shirt tucked flat into his pants. Cash couldn't find so much as a stray dog hair or misplaced button. He was neatness, itself. And that terrified Cash, reminded him of men he'd known growing up: men immaculate on the outside and rotting within.

The man stood before the door, hands on his hips, scanning the strip mall parking lot with furious purpose. When he spotted the trouble, half-hidden behind a stucco pillar, it sent a wave of panic clawing up Cash's spine. Was he about to be berated? Attacked? Asked to leave? *Hey kid, fuck off already*, or *Do you want me to call the police?* A call for help was always a threat. Cash took a deep breath and pulled the Jack Russell in his arms tight against his chest.

"Hi, sir," said Blue-tie, approaching without hesitation. "Can I help you?" The man was on the verge of middle-aged, with crow's feet flanking his eyes and silver creeping through his hair. Still, he called Cash *sir*. Cash didn't know what to make of that—feigned respect or condescension.

"Are you a doctor?" Cash had to force the words from his mouth. He now waited for the inevitable *I'm sorry, you can't be here*, knowing it would break him.

"I am. Who's your friend?"

Cash winced, the response too unexpected. "This is Jack. He's sick." Cash freed one hand to wipe his cheek before it darted back.

The doctor reached out gently and rubbed Jack's head. "Hey, Jack! I'm Doctor Burke." Jack eyed him curiously but otherwise didn't move. He grumbled when the doctor withdrew his hand.

"He says nice to meet you..." Cash muttered.

"What's been wrong with him?"

"He's not eatin..." said Cash. "Then this mornin I couldn't get him to follow me, so I picked him up, but he just fell over. He can't move at all, and I don't have any money or nothin', but I can work. I can brush animals or clean up after em— whatever it takes, I'll do it, you just tell me and I'll do it!"

The doctor raised his hand. "It's okay. Just *breathe...*" Cash didn't argue; he took a breath, and it rattled like loose change all the way down. "Let's not worry about that right now, okay? Let's just take care of Jack. What did you say your name was?"

"Cash," he admitted begrudgingly. The doctor made a face like he misheard him. This was not uncommon. People thought it was a joke. An irony concocted while high. "Like, *Johnny* Cash," he explained.

It was Cash's mother that had named him; she'd always loved the artist more than the arts. When asked why she didn't just name him Johnny, she told him, "Everyone's named Johnny. Nothing special in Johnny. It was always either *Cash* or *Sue*, and your father wasn't about to raise no queer." Cash had long wished they'd gone with Johnny. *Nothing special.*

"Oh, cool!" said the doctor, smiling with straight white teeth. "Well, Cash, why don't you bring Jack inside? I'll take a better look at him there."

The doctor turned back inside, and Cash just stood there paralyzed. Good things were rare enough, and life experience had taught him not to trust them. *There's no cleansing grace but rain,* his father used to say. *And even that can kill you.* Cash felt the fear tugging his arm to go. The soles of his feet itched to leave. But then a wet tongue licked his hand; a soft head nestled in the crook of his arm.

A blonde woman in green scrubs locked the door behind them. She avoided eye contact as they walked past, even when Cash startled at the sharp clack of the bolt. The woman smiled, though not at him.

"Do you want me to wait?" she asked.

"Oh, this shouldn't take long..." said the doctor.

"Thank you! Thank you so much..." said Cash, knowing words were not enough and yet he had nothing else. *Or do I...* he wondered. *Nothing good comes free.* How many times had his father tried to beat that into him? Cash only ever learned the hard way.

The doctor led him down a long hallway, past a never-ending series of closed doors, each one concealing a perfectly useable room, or so Cash figured. They passed an open area where anxious dogs barked from cages and technicians prepped syringes.

An old chocolate lab rose slowly in its cage, opened its mouth to bark, but the sound that escaped was only, *"I love you!"*

in a tinny, electric voice. Cash startled at that, and stopped.

"Voice box implantation," said the doctor casually, as though that explained all. He gestured Cash onward.

"*I love you! I love you! I love you!*" said the labrador as they walked away, but the hair raised on its back said otherwise.

At the very end of the hall, a door hung partway open. No light came from within. "In here," said the doctor. Cash wondered if it was an order. He stepped inside anyway, waiting for the light, or else the curtain to draw. For it all to be a joke. A trap. For the rug to be pulled out from under him and take the whole world with it. *Wouldn't be the first time...*

The doctor stepped in behind him.

Click!

And then there was light. Sterile, florescent light. The room was barren, save for a hand-washing sink and stainless steel table. Utilitarian in the extreme with one exception. On one of the vast beige walls hung a small painting: yellow dogs running through green fields, circling a red barn under a blue sky. Everything was in primary colors—simple, unjaded things. It was all very bright and happy.

It was also a lie, thought Cash.

Any moment now, the walls would come alive and swallow him. Undercover cops would appear and arrest him for loitering, for drugs, for disappointing his parents. Men in hazmat suits would charge in, restrain him, and drag him away to be experimented upon. No one wonders about the missing homeless.

The doctor shut the door. Was that a lock he heard?

"Why don't you set him there?" The doctor pointed at the table.

Despite his nerves, Cash didn't argue. He laid Jack gently across the table and stepped back, standing rigid as a scar while awaiting the next command or question. The doctor snapped into his blue latex gloves. *Primary colors*, thought Cash. *Lies...*

The doctor probed Jack's ears, listened to the whisper of his heart, molested him with rubber fingers. Cash watched the doctor closely for sign of trouble or recognition, for some perverse grin or an *Ah-ha!* But the doctor's eyes were too far away to read, as if they were looking at the space between Jack's molecules—analyzing, scrutinizing, dissecting.

"Are you a musician?"

It took Cash a moment to realize the doctor was speaking to him, not Jack. "I'm sorry?" he said, wondering how he had known and whether the doctor had just revealed his hand.

"The guitar..."

Cash had nearly forgotten about the battered acoustic slung across his back. "Oh," he said, feeling so foolish he nearly smiled before catching himself. "Yes."

The doctor grinned and continued the exam, occasionally muttering soft assurances to Jack, who panted and licked his lips. "What sort of music do you play?" said the doctor.

"Uh... Folk songs. Classic rock. I guess." Keep it short, non-committal, thought Cash. People do all kinds of things with personal information, and music was both his income and his passion, the addiction that fed his addiction. The thing that lifted and crushed him. Like teeth, he supposed.

"That's great!" The doctor smiled at him, warm and kind. "Like Bob Dylan, the Stones?"

At their mention, Cash was triggered. So few wanted to talk music with him anymore—about the messy purity of Richards and Jagger, or how Bob Dylan was a prophet straight from Heaven. Cash's walls tumbled down without him even realizing the earth was rumbling.

"Yeah yeah! Stones, CCR, The Doors. Me and my friend Donald play on street corners, and we try to put our own twist on em, you know, cuz you can't just play it straight without a full band. You gotta get creative to make the sound big and full, but when you think of those really great artists, it's usually just one or two people that made it great, you know, so like, why not simplify their—"

"Would you mind playing something?" asked the doctor, staring deep into Jack's eyes.

"What?" Cash was suddenly aware of how much he'd given away. He felt the heat of every bulb boiling microbes on his skin.

"A song. If you don't mind."

"Is that, uh... allowed?"

"Sure! Why not? Jack seems tense. Might calm him down."

Cash sensed a trap in this, but with Jack helpless and immobile in the doctor's hands there was no point in questioning. He swung the guitar around his shoulder. "Any, uh, requests?"

"What does Jack like?"

Cash smiled without realizing it. He gripped the guitar's neck, strummed the opening riff to "Have You Seen the Rain," and soon his voice cut through the chords with that classic Fogerty twang.

With Cash distracted and relaxed, the doctor continued his exam. He snapped his fingers in front of Jack's eyes, measuring their reactions. Jack blinked belatedly and jerked his head. "Has Jack had any recent head trauma?" asked the doctor.

Cash stopped just before the final chorus and stuttered, the guitar hanging in his arms like a dead thing. He didn't want to tell him about the fight he got into with another homeless person. Jack had jumped into the fray, tearing clothes and flesh and catching a wild punch for his trouble.

"He got in a tussle, yeah. With a dog, yeah."

"He may have brain swelling," said the doctor. "That would explain the gradual paralysis."

"Oh." Cash didn't know what to make of *brain swelling*. Was that a cancer-thing? He imagined Jack's brain blowing up like a balloon, pushing against his skull until it popped.

"That seems the likeliest possibility, though there are other, *rarer* maladies as well." Cash stood frozen, listening helplessly. "Fungal infections, slipped disks, brain tumors—Hell, it could be depression?"

"Depression?"

"Yes. It's not just for people."

"So what do I do?"

The doctor stepped back, hands on his hips, considering. "Well, normally I would suggest an MRI to give us a better sense of what's causing this sort of debilitation. Unfortunately, we don't have an MRI scanner. We're still fairly small and scanners are—as you might imagine—quite expensive."

"I understand." Cash didn't understand. Here they treated animals with cybernetic limbs and pets that were made of other pets. How was this so different?

"The good news is it doesn't change our first course of action. I'm going to give you some anti-inflammatories. If it is brain swelling, this should help Jack recover. If not, it won't hurt him, and we can go from there."

Cash was speechless. Indeed, he could barely breathe. This was more than he'd dared hope. His face felt like a black hole, everything collapsing towards the center in sudden relief. Unbidden tears streamed down his face, forming brown specks on the floor. He dug desperately through his pockets for a napkin or handkerchief.

"It's okay," said the doctor, walking over and placing both hands on Cash's shoulders. "I'm glad to help. But I want to make one thing clear: I wouldn't normally release a dog in this state. He should really be at an intensive care facility. Now, my hope is that this will make him feel better and he'll gradually start to recover... But you should consider how you want to move forward if he doesn't improve."

"Oh."

"Listen, I don't want you to worry any more than you're doing. But if it comes to the point that Jack isn't getting better and he still won't eat, just know that you can bring him here and we'll help him pass on peacefully. Okay?"

Okay? That's how the exam went. At once an affirmation and a question, an ellipsis. Some crisis resolved, some threat left hanging. *Okay...* Cash felt anything but. *Come back and we'll kill your dog*, they said. *Okay?*

Home was a small park tucked within the curve of the Watt Bridge onramp. Their sleeping bag was laid along the cement wall so that no passing cars or dog-walkers could see or harass them. No one could tell them to leave or go home. That made this home, Cash figured.

Not so very long before, Cash had migrated nightly from couch to couch. At the very least he'd have a pillow and blanket on somebody's floor. But it was hard doing that with a dog, and harder still since he split with the friends he got high with. It was just the two of them now. He looked out for Jack and Jack looked out for him. Better to be clean in the gutter than dirty in the house, though even that sometimes proved too much.

Cash laid against the bushes that blocked out the wind, with Jack curled up beside him. They'd given the first pill back at the office, but Cash worried it had been too late. A hundred questions crept like cockroaches from the shadows of his mind. What if Jack died in his sleep? What would he do with the body? What would he do with himself? And the worst of them wasn't a question at all, but a hard certainty: he would get high.

It was a comfort cold as anything, but at least it numbed him, removed him from the terror of all this. Cash could go back to being a junkie. He had little enough, but he had that—a backdoor escape that was always near to hand no matter how far he ran. It was either that or face the grief that gnawed his heart like a worm through an apple.

Cash stroked Jack's black and white fur, whispering to him words of love and warmth until his speech slurred and his eyelids grew heavy. *"It's okay, skinny cow… You're okay…"*

Several times he startled at some screech of tires, worried Jack had yelped in pain as his heart gave out. Cash only got back to sleep once reassured by the gentle rise and fall, rise and fall of Jack's breathing.

All through the night, Cash shook from the cold and the fear. His dreams were fierce but vague, shadows dancing and blending together. They kept him panicked, kept him trembling and confused. One moment, he floundered and drowned in a cold, roaring current; the next he was carried by an angry mob, their raised torches singeing his flesh. Here he was lost; there he was ferried helplessly away, as impotent in his dreams as in the waking world.

But in the morning, Cash awoke to a wet nose sniffing his face, and it almost made him cry. His companion stood on all fours, as stable now as he'd ever been.

"Jack!" Cash rolled him to his side and kissed his head, while Jack's tail *smack, smack, smacked* the soft earth beneath them. Cash repeated his name again and again, and each time Jack's head swiveled toward him, panting, smiling. A blessed light had shown, and all the fearful questions now scurried back into their shadows, invisible in the black of his mind, to watch and lurk and wait.

"So dey juss gayoo sum druds, uh?" said Donald, another homeless musician plucking his way from meal to meal. He grinned at Cash, who felt uncomfortable despite trying not to. "Spose ah shuh git a dog too." When Donald spoke, all the gravel and dirt of the streets came up through his voice.

"Not those kinda drugs." said Cash, distracting himself by rubbing Jack behind the ears.

The afternoon sun had baked cement and asphalt into a steamy haze, but they'd found some respite in the shade of an empty alleyway.

"Lemme seeyum," said Donald, hand outstretched. Long dark hair hung in inky clumps over Donald's weather-beaten face, melting into a wild thicket of facial hair flecked with debris. But all of this could not hide the grin, nor the mischief fire in his eyes.

Cash tensed. "They're for Jack," he said, hoping it sounded firm. "They're makin him better."

"Ah juss wanna see," Donald insisted, unblinking. He set his guitar in the felt-lined case beside him, his glare striking bone-deep. Who could guess what those eyes unearthed when they squared on you? What weakness, what fear? Cash handed over the small blue bottle. Donald didn't bother reading the label. He popped the tab and fingered through. "Aw hell..." he said. "Ah cun tay dese."

"Don't," said Cash, clutching the worn neck of his guitar.

"Yoo don ian wanna try? Look a' Jack, man! If dese cun mae im bettuh, juss tink wha dey can do fah us! Open new wirls, new chore progressuns, rhyddms, melodees!"

"Doesn' matter..." said Cash. "Those pills are for Jack."

Donald appraised him through the dark strands of hair that glued to his face and, once satisfied, offered a mere chuckle. It was all just a joke. Just play after all. "Ey, man. Ya don' wanem, ya don' wanem." He handed back the pills.

Cash stuffed the bottle back into his pocket, grateful to have avoided conflict. But when he glanced up, he caught Jack watching him with sharp, unblinking eyes that sent a tide of shame rolling over him.

Somehow, Jack understood what was happening whenever he and Donald got high. He'd whine pitifully, passing worried glances between them. Sometimes this was enough to fortify Cash's resolve. To tell Donald no and mean it. But other times, Cash would look away, and for a few hours find a more complete relief than any other. It was a hard thing to refuse when the world was at turns too hot or too cold, and always stingy with its blessings. But when Cash came out of the fog, he always found Jack lying head down, eyes glazed and unwilling to meet him.

The look Jack gave him now was different. It was as if he were studying Cash, absorbing him in some vague but obvious way.

Donald plucked the open strings of his guitar from e to E. "Leds stot," he said, ever the one to lead. Donald strummed a percussive, palm-muted rhythm that invoked the intro to "Sympathy for the Devil." Cash quickly followed, finger-picking both the piano and bass lines in one unified melody.

Though Donald's speech was nigh unintelligible, when he sang his voice reached beyond language, tapping into some incommunicable ache that throbbed at the core of all living things. Cash, himself, was not without his talents: at turns making a guitar drip with heartache and longing, or charging the air with rowdy, joyous chords. He was digging into the lead when Donald called a stop.

"Wassee doin?"

Cash glanced up and found Jack thumping his paws fitfully against the ground. Terrified, Cash stopped playing.

Was this a seizure? A stroke? He jumped to his feet, and Jack followed.

"Jack! You okay, skinny cow?!" Cash feared this odd behavior was a symptom of something new bubbling to the surface, but Jack just smiled back at him, panting happily. "Why'd he do that, you think?"

"Ah dunno, man. Look lite he drummin. Ya say dere wuh awl dat shit iniss brain—"

"Swellin..." said Cash distantly.

"Yah, wull mayee now dat dass gone heez learnin frum you. He wanna play, man, leh im play." Donald dug through his mismatched belongings and withdrew a beat-up pair of bongos. "Ere, man. Lettum play withis." Donald set the bongos in front of Jack who sniffed at them, then looked up to Cash. "Play, man! Play!" Donald encouraged. "Giffussum tunes!"

Cash knew better than to trust Donald's ramblings, but right now he needed the odd distraction. Some simple answer to the questions that hounded him. He strummed the chorus of "Wayfaring Stranger" and Jack thumped his paws discordantly against the bongos, just as Donald suggested.

"Eez geddin ih, man! Eez geddin ih!"

Cash watched, amazed. Jack's timing was off, but he was close, which is nearer than most first-timers, and Jack was also a dog. Cash stopped playing, and Jack sat still.

"I toll you, man. Dem druds opun up the mind! Ere, tae duh bongos. Yoo neum mo den ah do rye now."

At first, nothing happened. Cash had left Donald shortly before dark and spent the early evening "home," trying to teach Jack how to play bongos. Cash played his guitar, something with an easy rhythm, but Jack just stared passively. "Come on, skinny cow..." Cash muttered.

Jack whined back at him.

The night was growing late. Already the city slept and dreamed. A lazy wind yawned through the park. Cash rubbed the weariness from his eyes, but found them no less heavy, and his fingers were growing sore.

Cash lifted Jack's paws and physically pressed them against the skins. Jack whined and sat back down. This was ridiculous, Cash thought. He picked his guitar from the ground beside him and began plucking another melody from its strings.

The song was new to him, something sweet and light. But it kept urging him quicker, calling for the panicked clamor of chords between the finger-picking. His easy glide across the guitar's neck became frantic, his hands clawing, clutching, running across the neck.

Up and down and to the sides, the song pulled him—quicker, quicker—as if it were trying to get somewhere. His hand was a raft drifting helpless down the neck, singing its narrow path around discord and calamity.

Cash was so focused on navigating the song he didn't catch when the bongos came in. They popped, cracked, and snapped with life. They gave a perilous timing, like the river of song was urging him towards a fall. The finger-picking turned to hard, crunching chords. But soon even they were blending—sliding and hammering and crashing together.

Together, he and Jack twisted through the melody, pulling something somber and forlorn from its sweet beginnings. They played until Cash grew tired, when the chill of pre-dawn numbed his fingers and only the tears warmed his face. The song ended on a precipice, its fall unwritten—or else, just a bit further downstream.

Cash sighed, wiped his eyes and looked to Jack who watched him curiously, then ran one paw over his own face.

The next day Cash showed Donald all that Jack had learned, and Donald sat back with a smile and said, "Wuh godda drummuh." They practiced all afternoon, tucked away in a dank but undisturbed alley, running through their most popular songs until Jack developed a beat for each one.

Cash showed Jack a few tricks and soon his rhythms became more intricate, his paws crossing over and under each other. He watched the humans carefully as they strummed and plucked their strings. And they watched him also.

Donald laughed between verses, delighted by their new gimmick. Occasionally, he'd change the words and sing his joyful thoughts to Cash. He'd sing of Jack's focus and how you could almost see the wheels turning behind his eyes.

Cash smiled and nodded while he played, but he didn't see any of that. He saw eyes that never blinked or looked away. Eyes that gave nothing—only took.

Around five o'clock, the traffic outside the alley started to pick up, and Donald announced they were ready. "C'mon," he said, grinning. "Almose appy our."

They found a street corner along a popular bar block and claimed it. Occasionally they'd see some other hopeful street performer pass by. "*Kee moothin...*" Donald would growl at them, and Cash was simultaneously grateful and shamed to have Donald there, standing on his side.

Before they started, Cash took Jack into a nearby coffee shop to bathe in the bathroom sink. When a nervous barista stepped up to address him, Cash quickly said, "He's a service animal!" Donald had once told him that businesses couldn't refuse you with a service animal. They couldn't ask for proof or documentation either. They just had to take your word for it. Often enough, this worked, though Cash learned not to try the same place twice.

Cash rinsed his face, arms, and hair. He tried to scrub out the stains in his clothes with little to no success. One thing he'd learned over the years: no one wants to look poverty in the face. The less homeless you looked, the more money you made.

He scrutinized himself there before the mirror. Wondered if he looked truly homeless, or just disheveled, if he was "put together" now. Either way, he felt lighter without the weight of the world's refuse on his shoulders.

He gave Jack a once over with warm water, which Jack groaned passively about. Before they left, he held Jack under the hot air dispenser to dry him off.

"Ya luhk good," said Donald once they emerged.

"Thanks," said Cash, smiling like he'd finally washed out a stain that had stuck to him for years.

"Ah's talkin ta Jack!" Donald had a good laugh at that.

Cash set Jack against the wall of a building and placed the bongos in front of him. He and Donald stood on either side of Jack, guitars slung around their necks like some fateful albatross.

The first piece they played was an old Irish folksong. Donald started off slow and melodic with a thick, husky voice that was made for open fields and foggy days. Then Cash joined in, strumming hard and heavy, and with him was Jack, sitting upright and thumping his skins, as wild and crackly as fire.

People were drawn almost immediately. They stopped from their walks and were late to their dinners and dates. Meanwhile, all three of them dug into the music, grinning like mad ghosts. Jack even bobbed and swayed, just like Cash.

They played old classics and songs they'd written. People sang along to the ones they knew, and a brief community formed there on the streets. Between songs, there was laughter and applause, cheers and flashes of light.

Afterwards, people approached Cash, wanting to know what kind of pet-mod he'd gotten for Jack. *Was it implant or hormone treatment? What did they charge? Who's your doctor?*

Cash just smiled at all their questions and ideas. "Jack's an all-natural skinny cow," he told them proudly. "We don't mess around with those drugs and stuff." Even as he said it, Cash felt the lie of it. But for a moment, he enjoyed the lie—the *What if?*

Several people asked to have their picture taken with Jack. Cash said of course, but Donald cut in: "Pithuhs aw ten dollas." Money poured into the open guitar case, easy as that.

At the end, Donald's case was lined with bills and rattling with change. The two of them felt rich as kings. They ran their hands through it all, not bothering to count their plunder, just taking it in with their fingers and eyes. Jack circled around them, tail wagging. He barked gruffly to be included and threw his own paws in as well.

When they divvied up their spoils for the night, Donald claimed the larger share.

"I don't know if that's right..." Cash tried. "We're partners. And they paid to see Jack play."

"Thass rye," said Donald. "Mah bonjoes."

By the third night, people were waiting on the corner for them to arrive. Cash and Donald didn't know what to make of that, so they smiled uncomfortably, pushed through, and took their places—backs against the wall, as they always were. There was laughter and applause as they set up their instruments, and they didn't know what to make of that either.

Cash didn't like crowds. They made him nervous. In the susurrus of shifting bodies he thought he heard a whisper: *You don't belong.* But when the music started, that sound was stamped out. Jack's drumming popped and cracked and killed the whispers, and Cash dared allow a smile. There were plenty now to go around.

After the show—and the inevitable request for pictures—one man lingered behind. He was dressed in tan slacks, their fold lines raised and prominent, and a pale blue polo buttoned all the way to his neck. Cash recognized him immediately. He was what Donald called an "easy mark."

More than that, Tom Lord was a businessman. He introduced himself and told them he'd recently opened a café downtown. On Tuesday nights, they had live performers but only the bands' friends showed up, and they just took up seats. Tom Lord was in need of something special, something unique, something that would draw people in.

"What do you say, guys? I'd pay you, of course, and you'd get all the coffee you can drink!"

"Sounds great!" said Cash. He couldn't believe how things were turning around for him. At this rate, he could soon afford new clothes, he could get a job, he might finally get him and Jack off the streets. *Clean* was the word, the future he imagined for himself, and it burned at the back of his mind like a stage light.

But Donald shook his head. "Ah dunno ih thass rye fuh us."

Cash looked to him, confused. This offer was only good news for them. Cash wanted to speak up, to take charge, but instead he followed Donald's lead.

Tom Lord looked distressed. "Uh, okay," he said. "How about this! Free meals. Eh? We make a heck of a grilled cheese." He grinned ear to ear, as pleased with himself as his mother surely was.

Things only got better, thought Cash in disbelief. He almost shouted his excitement before Donald spoke again.

"See, da prawlum is, ya don' wan two shlubs lie us comin off da streets ta ya nice estabushmin."

Tom Lord squinted at Donald, as if that would make his words any clearer. "Ah, hmmm, isn't there a shelter you can go to...?"

Cash deflated; Donald would lose this for them. He considered jumping in, accepting Tom Lord's deal in spite of Donald. But if he did that, Donald was like to be spiteful back, to not show up at all, perhaps even demand Cash return the bongos.

"*Shelder?!*" Donald scoffed, waving his hand. "Man, I god shelder. I god shelder wih my oalady! Nehermye. Wuh goud." Donald stomped off, dismissing Tom Lord, and reluctantly Cash followed.

"Wait!" said Tom Lord desperately. "Commit to a few shows and I'll set you up somewhere. You can get clean and have a good night's sleep beforehand."

Donald stopped, so Cash stopped too.

"Eh, ah spoze tha's okay." He looked to Cash thoughtfully and nodded. Cash tried to hide his worry and excitement and nodded. Beside him, Jack nodded as well.

Easy mark or not, Tom Lord was smart enough not to rent an expensive suite on their account. Still, the small two-bed motel room was nicer than any they'd stayed in since making their way to the streets. They were given the room for two nights, one for each show they would perform. Originally, they would only have the first night, but Donald had successfully pushed for a second.

The afternoon before their debut, Tom Lord stopped by with a barber and dog groomer. "All right, boys," he said. "Let's get pretty!"

Donald was first to shower and get trimmed, and disappeared entirely once finished. Meanwhile, the freshly-scrubbed Cash sat with a towel wrapped around his shoulders, waiting patiently for his turn.

"How do you want it?" the barber asked him.

Cash wondered how best to say, *Not homeless.* "Clean?" he shrugged.

The cold steel was sweet on his skin, as were the warm fingers sifting through his hair. Cash couldn't remember the last time anyone touched him like that, or touched him at all, really. He shut his eyes and was so relaxed he near fell asleep. When, at the barber's gentle command, he opened his eyes, Cash didn't recognize the face that met him.

His greasy, twisted hair was cropped short against his scalp, with the top a thick sheen running from front to back. Seeing himself, Cash felt like a new man. Like all the ugly past, the addictions and mistakes now lay behind him. He was *this* —this image of normal. He had a job. He paid his bills. He went home at night. *Surely.*

"I don't have a tip…" he realized, embarrassed.

"That's all been taken care of." The barber gathered his things and left, and Cash felt like he took some part of him too. Some small dignity Cash didn't know he had until it was lost, like a crumpled dollar in a back pocket.

When Jack came trotting out of the bathroom, his white on black coat glistening and smooth, he startled at Cash's new appearance. A low growl built up to a bark.

"Jack! You can't do that here!" Cash walked over and scooped him up, and Jack lay rigid and uncomfortable in his arms. He sniffed Cash but didn't recognize the shampoo smell, and growled again.

Before Cash could scold him, the groomer emerged from the bathroom carrying a used towel and a bag of cleaning products. "Boy, he needed that," she said, wiping her brow with her forearm. "There was fungus growing in his fur!"

"*Homeless*," Cash shrugged with a grin.

She didn't think it was as funny as he did. Jack still growled, but shrugged as well.

Inside the West Ender Café, a packed house awaited them. Some of the faces Cash recognized—fans and friends that watched them perform on street corners. There was applause as they came in through the side door with Jack trotting behind.

Tom Lord introduced them, giving a name they'd never claimed or asked for: "Give it up for *Skinny Cow and the Street Rights!*" The room erupted with cheers.

Jack started them off with a bongo solo that created an uproar of excitement through the crowd. Donald and Cash came in together on guitar, strumming quick and sweet to Jack's rhythm, while Donald growled the lyrics to "Whiskey in the Jar."

Around them cameras clicked and flashed, people laughed, they clapped, and Cash felt so happy he near collapsed. His face was tingly and warm, his fingers blissful sore. He strummed away, digging into the music and singing along with Donald who glanced back to him, grinning pure and simple. They fed off each other's energy, until even Jack was barking behind them, inspiring gasps and cheers from the crowd.

Afterwards, Tom Lord approached them, giddy as can be. The café was so packed they had to turn people away at the door. He gave them each a hundred dollars in cash, which Donald claimed wasn't enough.

"I believe that's what we agreed upon..." said Tom Lord.

"Fells short ta me. Dey came fuh us," he said, gesturing his hand across the crowded room.

Cash was nervous, feared Donald might lose this for them after all, but he had to trust Donald. Who knows what they might come away with this time.

"Ah tink ih ya wan us ta come back, weh nee a lil more."

Tom Lord looked to Cash who looked to Donald who didn't flinch. A moment later, Tom Lord was counting fifty dollars into Donald's hand.

As they left, Cash applauded Donald's business acumen and asked for his share of the extra money.

"Wha?" Donald looked at him perplexed. "Ah raced the price, I tae duh cut."

They didn't talk all the way back to the motel. Once they got in, Cash couldn't take the quiet and went for another shower—his third that day. He lost all sense of time in there, with the water washing away all his discomfort and ache. The warmth and privacy let him process things without the accompanying stress.

And tonight he was coming to terms with being taken advantage of. It wasn't Donald that troubled him, but Tom Lord. Though they'd never met, he'd recognized the businessman upon sight. In another universe, their lives might have been switched. Either way, they still bowed to anyone that pressed. In Tom Lord, Cash saw all the qualities he disliked most in himself. All the weakness and fear and the pathetic struggle for control.

It had to change, he determined. He would make it change.

When Cash emerged from the bathroom, he found a woman dressed down to her underwear, lying on his bed, petting Jack, who lay beside her.

"Uh, hi," Cash managed to get out.

"Hi." She barely glanced up before turning away, bored.

Cash stood there, confused, not knowing what to say. Donald was missing, but a moment later the door beeped and swung open.

"Finally…" said the girl as Donald entered. "I've been waiting forever." She rolled away from Jack and sat slouched on the edge of the bed.

"W-who's your friend?" asked Cash.

"Aw, sahhy," said Donald, apparently surprised to find Cash standing there. "Dis Cyntia."

"*Cindy,*" she said, rolling her eyes.

"*Cinny.*" Donald smiled but wouldn't meet Cash's eyes.

"Well, did you get it?" asked Cindy.

"Sha dih, darlin." Donald withdrew a bag from his pocket and sat beside her on the bed.

Cash watched them, speechless and still like a piece of furniture. He looked to Jack, who watched them as well, sniffing the air for hint of what was in the bag.

"Ey, man. C'mon. Wuh godda celebrade. Geh in on dis."

"Uh, I dunno…" He thought a moment. "What is it?"

"Juss coke, man."

Just coke. When Cash was a teenager, he'd gone from coke to crack to heroin, and then back again, thinking if he turned to something less potent it would curb his appetite. No matter how he bounced between them it always ended in him strung out with a tube tied around his arm. Still, he wondered if there weren't some happy middle-ground.

Donald held up the bag to his nose and smelled it. He kissed his finger, dipped it in the bag, and rubbed it across his teeth. Beside him, Cindy or Cynthia leaned close, wrapping her arm around his and staring lustily at the bag, and Cash wondered: *Why shouldn't I take part?*

They were in a safe place, well off the streets. Shouldn't he enjoy himself? Hadn't he earned that by now? It was growing dark in Cash's mind, the cockroaches slipping from their shadows, one by one, to join and mate and spread. Cash stared at the bag in Donald's hands, considering, and just the consideration made him feel weightless and heady, ready to float over, another ghost searching for the light. But a sharp whining pulled him back to his body.

"I think your dog wants some," said the girl, glancing over at Jack who stood at the edge of the bed, whimpering. The girl laughed pathetically. Even her own jokes bored her.

Cash avoided Jack's eyes though. He didn't want to see the desperation, the plea he knew was waiting. Cash had already surrendered to the possibility—the *maybe just tonight.* If he didn't get high now the desire would linger in his skin for days. Jack fidgeted and growled, demanding Cash see him.

But I need it... Cash almost said aloud.

Jack watched him, unblinking, and barked.

"Ee cant do dat ere, man," said Donald, snorting a line from the bedside table.

Suddenly, the seductive hue of getting high turned sour. More dirty than alluring. Like he'd mistaken oil puddles for rainbows. Cash shivered for another shower—where he could be washed clean, or just washed away. Where the desire for drugs would run down the gutters and back down the drain. But there was Jack, caught between him and his addiction.

When Cash picked Jack up from the bed, the girl flinched as if he might come in for a kiss. Donald didn't even look over. Cash almost walked out the door then, returned to the curve of the Watt bridge onramp, leaving the room to Donald and his new friend. But as Cash turned to bow out, he thought once more of Tom Lord— and refused to be him in an instant.

"*YOU* can't do *THAT* in *HERE*," said Cash.

"Do whah?"

"Get high!" Cash hadn't intended to shout, but at least he now had Donald's attention. Jack squirmed uncomfortably under his arm. "You need to send Cindy outta here. And I want my money. We should be 50/50. I want my cut. Now! *Please.*"

Donald chuckled and set another couple of lines.

Cash stepped forward and threw his hand across the table, spraying white granules everywhere. Before Cash knew what was happening, he was knocked onto the other bed while Donald's fists smacked repeatedly against his cheeks. Jack flew over him, yelping as he hit the floor.

Cash didn't know when it stopped. His face throbbed and throbbed like tiny, endless blows. He just became aware he was sprawled across the bed, floating away. When the spinning and throbbing finally stopped, Cash lifted his head as much as he could to look around. Donald and Cindy were gone, with not but a smear of white powder across the nightstand betraying their existence at all. The room was quiet, lonely, and afraid.

"*S'okay, skinny cow.*" Cash slurred before slipping out. "*S'okay.*"

There was no response.

It was early morning when Cash awoke, feeling heavy and sore and hung over. He called for Jack, but Jack didn't come. He called again, feeling something was forgotten or out of place.

Cash rose slowly from the bed, the world spinning and wobbly. He braced himself against the wall until it stabled. "Jack?" he called. But there was nothing. He rubbed his head and called again. A *thump thump thump* came from the other side of the bed. Cash stumbled over quick as he could.

Jack lay on the floor, eyes scanning passively and tail smacking the carpet but otherwise unable to move. All across his body, thin white stalks broke through the fur.

Cash was speechless, the blood and breath fleeing his face to hide in some deep, dark place. He bent over Jack and stroked his fur, moving his lips and trying to find the air for words. "Hey, skinny cow..." His voice was like a whisper on the wind, something carried from very far away. "Donald!" he called. "We gotta get Jack to a vet!" But when he looked to the other bed he remembered that Donald had gone. Remembered the events of the night—why his head ached so sorely and the room felt so cold.

Cash was alone in this.

He scooped Jack in his arms and rushed him from the room. Jack didn't move, but Cash felt thin, spindly stalks slide over his hand, searching the lines and cracks in his skin.

"I need help!" Cash shouted through the lobby, and every suburbanite, technician, purebred, mutt, and mod-pet turned sharply in his direction. People pointed and stared when he walked through the door. They muttered in hushed whispers.

"Excuse me, sir," said a receptionist. He looked ready to lead Cash back out the door when he spotted the white fingers stretching everywhere through Jack's fur. He let out an exasperated breath.

"Okay folks," he said, stealing the room, "I'm sorry but I need everyone to escort their animals out, please. Yes, now. No, I'm sorry, this is not a joke." He directed Cash away from them, kept him sequestered.

Before the lobby had fully emptied, a technician in full hazmat suit appeared from the backroom. The suit was bright yellow. *Everything's okay*, thought Cash forcibly. The hazmat visor was blurry and reflected the fluorescent light, obscuring the face. Cash couldn't see if the technician was man or woman, if they smiled or frowned or had compassion in their eyes. They were just this *suit*.

Jack sat heavy in Cash's arms, and when the technician took him, the sudden relief left Cash feeling hollow, scooped out. The hazmat said something indistinguishable. Probably, *Wait here.* Cash just nodded, ran his hands through his hair, over his face, trying to find some purpose in his body to occupy himself.

Doctor Burke came out, looking concerned as clients rushed their pets out the door. "Cash?" he said, squinting. Cash nodded, figuring the doctor didn't recognize him with a haircut and clean clothes. He hadn't yet realized the right side of his face was swollen like a tumor, as purple as sunset. "*Are you okay?*" the doctor asked with alarm.

"They took Jack... He's got stuff growin..."

Time passed, or didn't. Like the world around him, time was all a blur. Cash wiped his eyes. He sat in one of the comfortable chairs uncomfortably. He hunched forward, then slouched back. He stood up. He paced. He sat back down.

He tried to lose himself in the television where men in suits scoffed at recent politics. He watched the technicians come and go hurriedly, making phone calls and printing charts. Outside the world chugged along, oblivious.

He was alone. Like a castaway on a barren island, contemplating the rough waters and dreaming of some chemical oblivion.

"Ey Cash, may ah sih wittew?"

Cash startled and turned. He hadn't noticed Doctor Burke approach. "What?"

"May I sit with you?"

"Okay."

Doctor Burke slowly lowered into the leather chair beside his. "How are you hanging in there?" he asked.

"Okay." It was the only thing Cash could say out without crumbling.

"Before we talk about Jack... Is everything else all right? Are you safe?"

Cash didn't know what to say to that. Right now he felt like the tide was lapping at his feet, calling him in, away from the rough and craggy landscape of survival. "O—" He choked before he finished, tears breaking from his eyes, nose, and mouth. Cash wiped desperately at his face. "Is he dead?" he finally got out.

"That's a difficult one to answer, actually. Cash, do you remember how we thought Jack might just have brain swelling, but I said it could be something else?"

Phycomycosis exemplum was a rare fungal infection that affected cats and dogs. Once rooted in the brain, it bypassed neural pathways, copying the behavior of organisms outside the host to better infiltrate a potential host-group. When fully matured, it spread through the rest of the body until its spores broke through the skin.

"So all that stuff he was doin... playin' bongos was just..."

"*Phycomycosis exemplum*," said the doctor clinically.

Cash thought to all the ways Jack mimicked him, all the ways his best friend seemed human. Now he was told that wasn't Jack at all but something even further from humanity. Some gross, mindless mockery of it.

"It's impossible to draw a sharp line between what was Jack and what was the infection. But for him to push through in the end would require a tremendous effort of will that we don't often see unless the animal feels threatened."

"What are they doin to him?"

"Right now they're sanitizing Jack, killing the fungus right down to the base."

"So he'll be okay?"

Doctor Burke's face grew long. He looked away. "Perhaps I haven't been clear. The fungus actually *replaces* the brain of its host. It becomes like a copy until it's time to spread. The good news is that, aside from a little confusion, Jack was probably never aware it was happening. But I'm afraid he's been gone for some time..."

Cash felt as though something heavy and important had collapsed inside him. His heart, he thought. But it couldn't be that. That still ached and beat and bled.

He stood up abruptly with nowhere to go, and just as abruptly walked towards where the hazmat had taken Jack. Cash didn't know where he was going or what he was going to do, but he pushed through door after door, past surprised technicians who said he couldn't be there and walls of caged animals who watched him quietly with fear in their eyes.

Doctor Burke ran after him, calling him back and discouraging technicians from getting involved.

Cash came to a dead-end at a large steel door, like a walk-in refrigerator with a big circular window at eye-level. "Cash, don't..." he heard behind him, but he ignored it. Peering inside, Cash saw Jack lying across a stainless steel table. The hazmat circled around him, spraying a white mist from something like a fire extinguisher.

Thin wisps of smoke rose from Jack's fur as the stalks crumpled into dust, leaving red holes freckled over his body. The tail wagged cruelly, thumping once, twice, before the technician sprayed it and it stopped for good.

Cash clutched his scalp, his nails digging into the skin. He needed to get out of there. He thought about finding Donald, losing himself for a while. He'd have to apologize, of course. Make amends. And then he could blast his brain, with all its dolor and woe, so far into oblivion that he wouldn't feel anything but a flicker of nostalgia for better days.

Before Cash turned away, his eyes caught his own reflection, saw the hopelessness and grief and the red welt that bloomed across his face. That's what Donald's friendship had brought him. Suddenly, getting high never felt so low. Going back was just as empty as staying put.

The world lost all sense after that. Time and space fused together or broke entirely apart. He was weeping under florescent lights; he was on the streets alone; he was in the cursed room with Donald and Cindy. People were there beside him one moment, gone the next. Disembodied hands pat his back, led him elsewhere. Stray voices whispered like ghosts.

Every squeak of metal or rubber sole scuffing the floor sounded to him like a yelp, making him turn sharply in search for Jack, only to realize his mistake—the void that now awaited him.

It made that last memory come bubbling up through the grief—Jack standing on the motel bed, begging him not to get high. It was a memory that scared and shamed him. So much hung on the precipice of that moment, and yet all he wanted was to go back to it. If the fungus' goal was to fit in, why hadn't Jack just gotten high with him? Why couldn't they just share that together, him and Jack transcending time and space and all their troubles on a chemical journey?

Doctor Burke's words now came floating back to him: ...*to push through in the end would require a tremendous effort of will...*

The realization struck him sudden and unexpected, like garbage thrown from a passing car. The last time Cash saw Jack —the *real* Jack—he was pushing through the fog, doing what he always did for Cash: calling him back from folly. To now go back to Donald, back to the drugs, would be to dishonor this final act. Maybe even his life entire.

"I know this can't be easy for you," said Doctor Burke, appearing beside him. "But with this rare infection in town, there will be others. There will be pets that are scared and families that don't know what to do. We're going to be very busy trying to manage this, and we're going to need help —*lots of help*—taking care of them all. We're going to need someone on staff that understands what's at stake... Someone that cares. Maybe someone looking for a second chance..." He put a warm hand on Cash's back, and for a moment, the world was just a little bit less cold.

In the weeks ahead, sleep was hard to find. Like his prayers to the beyond, it rebuked all his efforts to connect. Though Cash now had a job, a room, a bed, their comfort was too alien to soothe his heartache. At night, he'd toss and turn, shift pillows and blankets about himself, and finally he'd consider sleeping on the streets just to feel a little closer to home.

The cravings kept him anxious, kept him fidgeting and uncomfortable. And the relief was still out there, somewhere, waiting for him. Always ready to take him back, to swallow him and all his grief if he only surrendered. The thought made him ill.

Once sleep finally came, it swept up and dragged Cash away like a current roiling beneath the surface. Cash rarely slept deep enough to dream, and often assured himself he hadn't dreamt at all, only fell into a black stupor. But occasionally he would startle awake, sure he heard Jack whimper, or yawn, or bark, and he'd accept then that he had indeed been dreaming, and dreaming, no less, of Jack.

In that moment, the distance between them didn't feel so far. Cash felt at once comforted and heartbroken then, aching for that connection that seemed so close he swore he heard Jack snuffling before realizing it was just the damp, sweaty sheets sliding over his body. He wept like he only had as a boy—breathy, voiceless, and trembling. Then, freshly exhausted, he curled up with pillows and sheets, shivered once for the warmth they couldn't give, and slept, and dreamed, and recovered.

A question for the author

Q: What's your favorite story?

A: I really love stories about reluctant friendship, where two enemies are forced to work together and over time they begrudgingly start to care. Begrudgement isn't appreciated enough in modern friendships.

About the author

Hamilton Perez is a writer and freelance editor living in Sacramento, California. When not writing, he can be found rolling 20-sided dice or chasing squirrels with the dog. He is also an Associate Editor at *Podcastle*.

hamiltonperez.wordpress.com, @TheWritingHam

Cathedra

M.C. Tuggle

We glided out of the base's garage onto smooth tarmac, but once we hit the icy terrain, things got bumpy. The rover shimmied up a rise pocked with shallow fissures and slowed to a crawl as we neared the crest. I gazed up. Saturn and its massive rings dominated the sky, glowing in the dim bronze light of early morning on Enceladus.

We stopped. Rafferty tapped my shoulder from the rear seat. I was so absorbed in the view she startled me. I turned, and for an awkward moment, we were face to face. Through her crystal-clear helmet, glints of simmering anger flashed in green eyes set off by a mop of red hair. She pointed to a smooth stretch of grey ice in the gorge below and said, "That's it, Kaplan. That's where our friends were working. They never had a chance."

Beside me in the driver's seat, Martinez turned his dark eyes on me, his head tilted back. "Yeah, that's the spot. 'Safe for geothermal drilling,' according to the survey."

Our helmets were equipped with automatic radio comms, as well as audio sensors and external transducers for through-water comms, but I didn't answer. Martinez sat back and kicked the brake. The rover purred down the slope as Martinez jerked the tiller left and right to dodge ice blocks in our way. Even in the tiny moon's low gravity, our loopy course threatened to hurl us out of our seats. My companions seemed to have no difficulty. I tightened my grip on the grab bar.

Martinez shot a look at me. "Better hold on, Kaplan."

The way Martinez was driving, and with no protective sides on the rover, I could've been flung out onto the rock-hard ice. In fact, my two associates might've been hoping to see me take a fall, since everyone on Cassini Base blamed me for the disappearance of two of their coworkers.

Well, that's me. Always the odd man out.

The three of us, me, Martinez, and Rafferty, the electrician's mate, wore white company-issued biosuits, easily the best I'd ever used. They'd been designed to function on surface and underwater, though powerful, shifting currents made it impossible to work in the underground seas. In addition to flex-ballast to simulate 70% g, the suits supplied us with air, and were enviro-adaptable and armored to protect us from Enceladus' hostile environment. So if the journeyman astrogeologist tumbled out of the rover, no one would be reprimanded. In fact, it'd make a great story back at base.

We reached smoother terrain and coasted toward a dozen or more toppled ice columns that looked like a collapsed Stonehenge. Something caught my eye and I twisted around. On the grey horizon, a geyser shot superheated water into space, followed by another. Seconds later, the twin rumbles reached us through the moon's thin atmosphere, registering nearly 50 decibels in my suit's audio sensors. The fountain-like spray rose high, caught the sunlight, and formed a gigantic sparkling cone with Saturn looming in the background like an enormous round agate of gold, blue, and white bands. Most of the propelled water would add to the moon's atmosphere, but some would break free of Enceladus' gravity and become part of Saturn's E ring.

We reached the site where the two men had vanished. Martinez braked the rover, and we clambered out. Rafferty busied herself setting up the 3-D imaging unit we'd brought from the main base, and Martinez followed close behind me.

There was no doubt in my mind that both watched my every move.

The terrain surrounding us was warped and striated with pressure faults, smooth in places, powdery in others. Blunt ice boulders and smaller chunks littered the area. And there it was – in the center of a stretch of ice otherwise smooth as glass, ten feet of a silent drill derrick poking out.

When I turned toward Martinez, he wasn't looking at the accident site. His eyes had narrowed on me.

He nodded toward the drill. "Hasegawa's comm is still active down there." Martinez' tone was icier than the atmosphere. He took a deep breath. "We never heard from Spenser. And that's been almost three months."

"How do you know it's still active?"

Martinez patted the back of his suit. "When you put in a charged lithium pack, your suit is operational about four months, including the radio. The three of us are sending and receiving on frequency Tac 12. But if an activated suit is not in motion more than three minutes, it's assumed you're in trouble, and a dead man circuit kicks in. The helmet comm receives all live transmissions so you can locate help, and broadcasts a directional beacon on the emergency frequency."

Yep. Damn good biosuits. The company takes care of its own.

I recalled this spot from when I conducted my original survey nearly a year ago. We stood at the moon's south pole, one of the most complex and tectonically active regions in the solar system. Enceladus was covered in water ice that hid a liquid sea and hydrothermal flows heated by tidal friction and radioactive decay. The company that had hired me, Xtracta, planned to tap into the moon's vast geothermal reserves and ship charged supercapacitors to power-hungry space outposts. That plan had suffered a major setback when the two crewmembers disappeared. Which was why we were here.

I looked up. The alarm array on a utility pole near a small, nearby mound of dark ice showed no sign of damage. I tapped the touchpad on my wrist and studied the display in my visor. "Strange," I said. "All the sensors and alarms I installed are responding. Everything's working."

Martinez faced me, arms folded across his chest. "Well, Kaplan, then I suppose you're done here. You can go back to the belt and forget about us. Again."

I didn't respond. But something about Martinez' tone got to me. People like Martinez were one of the reasons I preferred working alone as an astrogeologist in the asteroid belt. The asteroid miners kept to themselves and paid well for my surveys. But when Xtracta contacted me about the disappearance of its two crewmembers, I'd felt I had to come back. It had taken nearly three months catching transports, but I was here to do what I could. What I had to do. Anyone who questioned my work was going to hear from me. I'd come back to defend myself.

But now a growing ache in my gut told me I might be responsible for the deaths of two men. An unknown geohazard must've killed them – unknown because I had overlooked it. Nothing else could explain what had happened. The football-sized creatures that raced in the small moon's sub-surface seas were harmless. Cute, even. The miners had dubbed them sea pigs.

My response to Martinez was to march out to the derrick. Martinez dropped his arms to his side and stared at me. Rafferty turned from the equipment she was setting up. Neither wanted to miss the sight of me crashing through the ice.

"It's solid here," I said, stomping my boot. "The alarms would go off if the ice was thinning or under stress." When I touched the drill's control panel, the unit's display lit up, and I squinted at it. The drill had punched through the ice and had penetrated rock, still several meters away from the superheated water that surged below the surface. But the display indicated the wellbore had ruptured. What the hell could've caused that? Squatting, I brushed away blue powder ice from the surface. The solid ice showed signs of stress and rapid re-freezing. "Has anyone tried to retrieve this equipment?"

Martinez remained motionless. "No one's dared. Not after what happened."

"I don't get it," I said. "There's no way hot streams from the interior could breach the surface. Not here. The ice is always at least 30 centimeters. And look at this." I pointed toward the drill's display, but Martinez and Rafferty didn't budge. "The wellbore is still embedded in rock. Don't see how enough hot water could've seeped out to do any damage." After another glance at the drill's display screen, I said, "Rafferty, let's roll out the GPR."

"Hooah." She turned half way, looked back at me, and scurried back to her equipment.

"As soon as the ground penetrating radar maps the interior, I should have a better idea what's down there, maybe even figure out what happened. Then we can power the drill back up and replace the bore."

"What's the map gonna show you?" Martinez folded his arms.

"Hopefully, that it's safe to continue."

Martinez snorted. "You're mighty cautious when it's your butt on the line."

"Yes, I am." I turned away, burning in shame. Why the hell had I said that? I leaned close to the drill's control panel. "There's the main power. If the area's secure, we can continue to drill, finish the job. The one thing we don't want to do is overlook–"

That's when the world I thought I knew disappeared.

A powerful shock wave whipped through my body, and the ice around me pinged and cracked and roared. Something tossed me high over the surface, and I tumbled and dropped among shards of flying ice. The alarm blasted the air, and the crisis alert chime in my suit sounded. I bellyflopped into water, and the instant I hit, something wrapped around me and pulled me down into darkness.

I rocketed through the water at mind-numbing speed. I tried to switch on my suit's light panel, but whatever was pushing me had pinned my arms back. Helpless and terrified, I sped face-first through black water.

Seconds later, as suddenly as it had started, all movement ended. I glanced around, panting. Blood throbbed in my ears. There was no sign of whatever had brought me here, and I drifted in the water. It took a few seconds to control my breathing and orient myself. I was in an underwater cave. My audio sensors picked up the dull thunder of water rushing through a nearby channel, broken every few seconds by the crash of a powerful surge colliding with rock. Several meters away, a dim light flickered through water thick with icy slush. By kicking my legs and pulling myself along the rocks, I glided toward the white glow that gave the chamber its only illumination.

I stopped. A figure in a white biosuit, arms and legs spread-eagled, stared back at me. But when I pulled closer, the suit's sleeves floated free in the current. They were empty. It was just a biosuit and its helmet wedged into the rocks, its fading light panel illuminating the watery chamber. The armor at the chest appeared gouged open. I switched on my own light panel and read the letters "HASEG." A cold shudder shot down my spine.

A voice in my helmet said, "Kaplan, do you copy?"

"Yes, Martinez, I copy."

"I've been trying to reach you. What happened?"

"Something dragged me underwater. What did you see?"

"Water, ice, arms, legs. Where the hell are you? You okay?"

"I'm in a cave, and I'm still in once piece. Martinez – I found Hasegawa's suit and helmet."

"Is he ..."

"There's no sign of his body. And I haven't seen any trace of Spenser." I switched off my suit's light panel. No telling how long I'd be stuck here, so I figured I'd better conserve power.

After a long pause, Martinez said, "What can we do?"

"Say again?"

"Kaplan, I repeat, what can we do?"

"Hold on."

Martinez' voice was echoing in my audio sensor, repeating what I heard over the comm. How was that possible? I turned up the amplitude on my through-water system and heard a team leader bark at workers in the hangar for not moving uncharged supercapacitors into the warehouse. Then I remembered what Martinez had told me about our suits. The dead man circuit in Hasegawa's comm system had triggered, so it repeated all radio conversations in the area.

It was possible a random burst of superheated water had broken the ice I'd been standing on and washed me into this cave. But what had stuffed the helmet and the suit in the rocks? And why?

"Martinez, do you copy?"

"I'm here."

"I'm going to look around, see if there's a way out. Rafferty?"

"Rafferty here."

"Go ahead with the 3D mapping. Look for an opening in the rocks."

"Hooah," she said. "Got it. And good luck, Kaplan."

"Thanks."

This seemed like a good time to check the indicators in my visor display. No telling what might be useful. Trimix replicator: fully functional, so I had plenty of air. Surrounding water: 7 Centigrade, but the suit's enviro regulators checked out. At least I wouldn't be frozen or cooked alive in this crazy stew of freezing and boiling water. Ambient radiation: now that was a problem. The radiation in the cave was high. Deadly high. Nearly 25 Sv. My heart sank as I did the math. I had less than an hour to escape.

Then another problem – the light behind me went out.

I nudged against the rock to turn around, and peered into murky water. Just as I started to power on my own light panel, I realized the light from Hasegawa's suit was still on. Something floated between me and the suit, blocking the light. Something large. And it was only a couple meters away.

This was serious. A breakaway ice column drifting in the powerful currents could crush me. I glanced around the cave searching for an escape route and realized my situation was even worse than I first thought: there were several enormous columns floating in the cave. The moon's wildly elliptical orbit created enormous friction between the ocean and the moon's rocky core, and that friction heated the underground sea. Other streams heated from radioactive decay blended with those currents. If heated waters from another region had shifted, my little underwater cave could suddenly freeze up, and the radioactivity would be the least of my worries.

The column nearest me moved. It didn't lurch in random current, it flexed so that it remained close to me as I drifted. It jerked closer, and when I tried to swim out of its path, it changed course until it was nearly in my face. And it had eyes.

Clicks and deep grumbles sounded through the audio sensors of my through-water comm system, which were answered by eyes opening on the dozens of other large shapes in the cave. The dim glow from the dead man's suit reflected red in the large eyes that surrounded me.

It took me a long moment to comprehend what I faced. These giants weren't friendly little sea pigs.

And here I was trapped in an underwater cave full of them. My heart thumped in my chest, and I took a couple of gulps of air. I had to remain calm. I let myself drift in the water, unsure how any effort to maneuver might be interpreted.

I could tell I was being studied by these aquatic creatures. The one closest to me was at least four meters long, with a thick, streamlined body that glistened like slate in the dim light. It resembled a dolphin with an alligator's thick hide. A row of spikes formed along the spine. Oval, reptilian eyes that blinked from front to back sat high on top of a cone-like head. The blunt jaws, anchored by a massive neck and chest, suggested monstrous power. The creature had two long flippers in front and stubby flukes on its tail. And near the tail, a thick dorsal tentacle swayed menacingly.

Was I in their dining room? Had Hasegawa's suit been mounted in the rocks as a trophy?

Radioactivity was accumulating in my body, so I had to do something. I needed a better idea of my surroundings, and how many mouths were aimed at me. I switched on my light panel at its lowest setting.

Rapid clicks and moans filled the cave. Like a school of fish, the creatures rippled away from the light, but as they retreated, each one formed a fist at the end of its dorsal tentacle. The balled-up tentacle reminded me of the hammer tail of the ankylosaurus, and I had no doubt of the immense power behind each.

The creature next to me nudged forward and faced me. My only weapon was the light panel in my suit. The max setting might blind the creatures. But only some. And then what would I do? I had no idea how to get back to the surface.

The creature opened its mouth, revealing three rows of pointed black teeth. A rapid pulse of clicks sounded from it. Adrenaline fired through me, but I forced myself to remain still and face whatever was about to happen.

Then the creature said, "Have you finished?"

All I could do was stare back. The creature's voice was a bone-rattling bass. I took a deep breath and switched on my external speaker. "Finished what?"

"Mourning your dead self."

I wrestled with a response, but gave up. "Please explain."

"Part of you died. You have seen the shell. The suit." It slowly shut and opened its red, slotted eyes. "Know that the dying was necessary."

So these creatures had killed Spenser and Hasegawa. A knot of fear clenched my stomach.

"How is it you can talk to me?"

It looked at Hasegawa's suit. "We listened."

That was another punch to the gut I wasn't ready for. This creature had learned to speak our language by overhearing the communications on Hasegawa's radio.

"That's – quite an accomplishment."

"We must speak to the beings who feed us, the podfrums, gallytrots, and firedrakes. What you would call our prey."

Predators. They fed on the smaller animals that lived in the underground sea. I had to force myself to breathe deeply. These alien beings possessed an intellect as breathtaking as their physical power. And they were apparently immune to extreme heat, cold, and radioactivity.

Were we considered a new prey species?

Surrounded by intelligent aliens of immense power, and my body absorbing radioactivity at dangerous levels, I had little to lose by interrogating them. More important, the crew at Cassini Base had to know what was down here. My finger tapped the control panel on my arm to transmit our conversation.

"Who are you?"

"We are Of Na. And you are Kaplan."

It had heard my name on Hasegawa's comm when I was talking to Martinez and Rafferty. There was no doubting its intelligence. "You said it was necessary the two men had to die. Did you kill them?"

Of Na blinked its eyes. "That horrid thing they brought to life, your drill, was harming Na, which would deprive Cathedra of her beauty."

"Who are Na and Cathedra?"

"Na is our home, what you call Base. Cathedra is the great One above. You call it Saturn."

"How do you know what's above?"

"We can see through the ice in many places, especially near the geysers. Sometimes pools form near the heated water, letting us look up at Cathedra and its holy circles. And we can open the ice when Na's currents allow us."

So that's what their hammer tails were for. I had to let Martinez and the others know what they were facing.

"Did you break the ice and bring me here?"

"We heard you tell yourself on the comm you were going to bring the horrid drill back to life. The Hasegawa and Spenser parts of you had to be stopped. And you, Kaplan, had to be stopped."

"Why? Why did you have to stop us?"

A long moment passed before Of Na shut its long eyes from front to back. Then it said, "You would have disrupted Na's lifeblood, which we offer to Cathedra.

When an offering is accepted, our dead become part of Cathedra's sacred rings."

It shuddered, edged closer, and its broad, powerful mouth hovered inches from my face.

"Your time of mourning is finished."

Before I could answer, the creature's tentacle shot forward and the sledgehammer on the end opened up and engulfed me. Darkness hit me like a falling rock, and we took off. The sudden g-force from shooting through water turned my brain to mush. Seconds later, we stopped. Too lightheaded to react, I drifted in total darkness. The distant roll of surging water rumbled in my through-water comm. I gulped air, found the control for the light panel in my suit, and peered into a pair of long, reptilian eyes. A panicked search of my surroundings revealed we were alone in a water-filled, rocky chamber.

Despite my suit's enviro-regulators, my entire body was slick with sweat.

I started to ask Of Na why it had brought me here, when a rat-like, rust-colored skeleton floated in the light from my suit. Following in its path were dozens of similar remains, some whole, with wide, staring eye sockets, and many others headless. A few meters away, at the fuzzy edge of my beam, a creature like Of Na drifted, its massive jaws gaping as it slowly cartwheeled in an invisible eddy.

"What you call the geyser will soon erupt at this place. We have honored the dead by bringing them here. What is left of their bodies will be sky-scattered."

The small skeletons must've been the sea pigs these creatures hunted. While that thought sank in, my still-addled brain comprehended what Of Na had just said: a geyser was due. In my survey, I'd concluded the geysers erupted irregularly, and other geologists had confirmed that.

"How can you predict a geyser?"

"We listen. We know." Of Na cocked its head and slowly blinked. "The Hasegawa and Spenser parts of you were also sky-scattered, and are now part of Cathedra's rings."

I glared back, so enraged my vision went blurry. "You killed them because they were drilling?"

"You are worse than the podfrums. Even they understand when we explain what has to be done." Of Na shuddered. "We had to stop you from destroying Na's lifeblood, which feeds Cathedra. We did not know you could be killed so easily." It shook itself, edged closer. "But you have said you will drill again, and we have pledged a sacred oath to protect Na. We will surround your mess, your barracks, your rec center, your garage, and your admin building and crush them."

My anger at the planned mass murder crowded out what the creature had claimed about the geyser. The roar and hiss of powerful streams of superheated water crashing against the chamber's walls reminded me, and I checked my visor display. I blinked, and looked at it again. The surrounding water was 98 degrees Celsius, approaching the boiling point.

My heart dropped into my gut when I realized the creature might be right about an imminent geyser. The blast from a geyser eruption would shred and atomize anything in its path. Including me.

Of Na turned around.

"Wait – are you going to leave me here?"

The creature did not face me, but rumbled its reply. "It is our way to give all a proper sky scattering. Whatever good or harm one has done, the story of their life must have a proper end."

My entire body tightened up. I gulped a breath of air. "Of Na."

No response.

"Of Na, you told me you can see Cathedra when the currents allow you to break the ice."

For a long moment, there was no reply. "Yes."

"I – *we* – don't believe you would wrongfully take life. But we don't know how to read the currents. If you told us where it is safe to break the ice and run our generators, there would be no harm to Na. Cathedra would continue to receive your dead."

Of Na turned until we were eye to eye. It gave me a long, slow blink – hopefully a good sign. For the first time since I'd crashed through the ice, the tension that had knotted my stomach relaxed, and I exhaled.

The creature regarded me without moving or speaking.

I said, "We can adapt the comm so you can use it to tell us where it is safe to drill."

Of Na cocked its head. "That would be – impossible, Kaplan."

"Impossible? Why?"

"We have listened to you argue among yourselves. You are too stubborn, too greedy to be trusted. You would not follow our instructions."

"But we would. We will shut down a turbine when you make your offerings. We can switch to different locations so we don't interfere with Na's lifeblood. I promise we will do as you say."

Of Na closed its huge eyes several moments. When its eyes reopened, it stared at me. "What you are saying is pure bullshit."

It had certainly paid attention to the crew's radio chatter. "Of Na, wait – you said you made a sacred oath to protect Na."

"Yes."

"We can make our sacred oath to you."

Of Na studied me without speaking. It opened its mouth and let out a loud stream of clicks. Its eyes opened and closed in a jittery, shaking motion.

Was this its version of laughter?

Not far away, rushing water thundered against rock, and the walls around us groaned. Bubbles fluttered up from the depths. The water was boiling. A glance at my visor display showed the water had reached 102 degrees.

The creature stopped shaking. "Kaplan, I have listened to you many sunrises. You are a contentious, divided people. There is too much mutual distrust for a sacred oath to have any meaning."

"Ah–" I stared back into those probing, alien eyes, my mind racing. There was no way to convince Of Na we could be trusted. And time was up.

Then it hit me.

"Yes, we do." I swam close to the creature's broad face. "We have a sacred oath, and you have heard it. What's more – you have heard us fulfill that oath."

"You really need to cut the crap."

"That oath, which we hold sacred, is –'Hooah.' When we make this oath, it is our duty to do what we say. I'm surprised you haven't recognized that oath for what it is."

The front flippers quivered, and Of Na backed away, its eyes locked on me.

"Of Na, if you destroy the base, more of us will come, and there will only be more damage to Na. Take me to the surface, and I will convince the others what they must do."

Of Na made no reply.

Deep below, something snapped, radiating shock waves through rock, ice, and water. I made the mistake of looking down toward the source. At that instant my head jerked back in my helmet and I plummeted through inky water, the light panel in my suit illuminating knife-like rock shards that flashed bright, then flickered into darkness. I spun at breakneck speed through tight channels of rock and ice, then raced through icy slush.

Suddenly, no more motion. A bone-shaking thump, followed by a metallic crash, and the next thing I knew, I was facing Of Na, who dangled me from its dorsal tentacle. We were nearly eye to eye, and the light from my suit cast deep shadows on Of Na's rock-like, muscular face.

"Kaplan, you will speak to me through the suit we possess before the next sunrise. We will then guide you to a place where you can safely drill."

Reeling and nauseated from hurtling through deadly waters, I held my head as high as I could, took a deep breath, and with my last trace of strength, firmly replied, "Hooah."

Of Na whipped his tentacle and tossed me.

I shot out of the water, slid several meters, and sprawled onto the icy surface. As I staggered to my feet, the flash-frozen water on my suit splintered and cracked in the freezing atmosphere. Lightheaded and stumbling, I searched my surroundings. When I found the place Of Na had hammered through the ice, it had already turned solid. It took a couple of drunken efforts to cut the power to my suit's light panel.

"Martinez? Do you copy?" In all directions, the frozen, twisted terrain stretched toward a black horizon, with no sign of help. "I'm on the surface. Martinez? Rafferty? Cassini Base? Can you hear me?"

A geyser flared and rumbled directly in front of me, shaking the ice under my feet, spewing a giant plume of water, silt, and the remains of dead, alien beings into space. The ice rattled and cracked, but I didn't have the strength to run. I gazed up at the gigantic spray as it caught the sunlight. Saturn, its huge rings nearly a knife edge, loomed overhead, glowing its warm colors.

Never again would I see geysers the way I used to. They were more than interesting displays. The creatures of

Enceladus – or should I say Na – were building something – something worth working for. Something worth defending. I understood.

Over the roar of the nearby eruption, Martinez' voice crackled in my helmet. "We've spotted you, Kaplan. We're at bearing 270, and on our way."

I scanned the area. The rover bounced and wobbled toward me at full speed over the rugged surface. Rafferty waved, signaling me to run away from the geyser. I plodded a few steps, slipped, and fell flat on my face. The groaning and trembling in the ice warned of the possibility of fissures opening around me. I pushed myself up on my arms and focused my remaining strength on scrambling to my feet.

Martinez scowled when he stopped the rover. "Damn, Kaplan, get in."

I hobbled forward. Rafferty grabbed my outstretched arm in both hands and hauled me into the back. She scooted into the front seat, and Martinez revved the engine and steered toward base.

The rich hum of the rover's engine turned into a whine as we gained speed. Flat on my back, arms and legs like jelly, I gulped air.

Martinez glanced back at me. "Took you long enough. That was a hell of a geyser blow. We coulda been launched into space."

I didn't say anything. A couple of minutes later, Rafferty turned toward Martinez and must've given him a look, but I couldn't see their faces.

"Thought you'd like to know, I relayed your comms when you were underwater so the whole base knows what happened to you down there." Martinez shifted in his seat, leaned back a bit. "And I just got a priority comm from the commander. After sick bay checks you out, I'm taking you to her office. She wants a full rundown on this deal you want to make with that creature."

I was too beat to answer.

"I wouldn't worry about it," said Martinez. "She's reasonable. And I shouldn't tell you this, but she did tell me we need someone who knows the crazy geology here, someone who can handle our underwater friends."

Rafferty pivoted in the passenger seat, tossing the mane of red curls inside her helmet as she faced me. "Know anyone like that?"

I gave her the strongest grin I could manage. "I'll ask around. But first, I'm taking a long, old-fashioned rest."

Rafferty raised an eyebrow. "I guess you've earned it."

I nodded agreement and shut my eyes and let my bruised body conform to the shape of the back seats. Maybe it was exhaustion, maybe it was the moaning engine harmonizing with the swift beat of the rover gliding over bumpy ice, but I thought I saw the mist from the heart of Na racing through dark space to merge with the rings of Cathedra.

About the story

"Cathedra" is a "hard-science" story, inspired by an article in *Astronomy* magazine on Enceladus, the most promising site for life in our solar system. It's a tale of faith and one's discovery of purpose within society. The title and theme came from this anecdote:

A man came upon a construction site where three people were working. He asked the first, "What are you doing?" and the man replied: "I am laying bricks." He asked the second, "What are you doing?" and the man replied: "I am building a wall." As he approached the third, he heard him humming a tune as he worked, and asked, "What are you doing?" The man stood, looked up at the sky, and smiled, "I am building a cathedral!"

A question for M.C. Tuggle

Q: What kind of non-fiction do you like to read and how does it affect the fiction you write?

A: I enjoy history, especially ancient and American colonial history. Articles on astronomy, evolution, and electronics always grab my attention, and often inspire story ideas.

About M.C. Tuggle

M. C. Tuggle is a writer living and working in Charlotte, North Carolina. In addition to fantasy, science fiction, and crime novels, his reading includes history, especially military history. An avid weightlifter, tennis player, and student of martial arts, he has been married to Julie Tuggle since 1982 and is the proud father of a daughter, Jessica. He blogs at mctuggle.com.

@tuggle_mike

The Cypress and the Rose

Sandi Leibowitz

On her sixteenth birthday, a girl approached her mother, a priestess gifted in prophecy, to learn her name and her fate. The trees of that island country spoke with the people, the priestesses most of all, and taught them things that we, to whom the trees are mostly silent, cannot guess.

"Your true name is Cypress," the mother told her.

"The tree of mourning?"

"The tree of resilience. It is long-lived. And where there is death, the cypress stands vigil, its life in balance with what's been lost. Your destiny, daughter, is to leave our land and find a tower of roses. Then, like a rose, the story of your life will unfold."

"What is a rose?" asked Cypress, for their island, rich in hibiscus, bougainvillea, and a thousand other flowers, had never known roses.

The priestess described them to her daughter, adding, "You must go east, to the crowded realms. That is what the trees tell me."

And so Cypress traveled across the sea, hiking deserts and ice caps, climbing mountains, sailing rivers. It took the better part of a year before she came to the place her mother had foretold: a castle with a garden famed for its rose beds, and more famous still for an ancient tower around which the roses were so thickly planted it was practically smothered in them.

She arrived in autumn, when most flowers were already dead. But the roses of the tower, even at their ebb, still blossomed in a cancerous surfeit of white petals, their perfume sickly sweet like pastries in a house of mourning. Despite those fulsome blossoms, the hedge was more thorn than flower. Cypress could understand the greenspeech of most plants, though trees spoke with the clearest voices and had the most to say, but from the great rose-hedge she heard only an angry humming, as of a hive of bees whose honey has been stolen.

Cypress asked for work and was grudgingly hired as a lowly scullery maid, only because the girl who'd last held that post had run away. The castle folk mistrusted the foreigner for her dark coloring, which they called ugly, though in her own land her cinnamon skin had been praised for its beauty. They thought her oafish and ungainly, for she was tall in the ways of her country-folk, a head or two above the tallest men in the east; the dress they made her wear barely reached her ankles, though it hid the strong legs she'd earned from a lifetime of swimming and running and the full skirts weighed her down, making her slow. The castle folk rarely spoke to her, even Myllem, the cook. Cypress bore all, for this was her fate, and she knew that happiness, or at least some great purpose, awaited her.

Only one other was treated worse. It wasn't Raffin the dim-witted stable boy, for he was Myllem's son, and even his stupidest mistakes were laughed off and forgiven. No, it was Rosabella, the princess.

Her milk-white skin had no bruises, and she was clothed and fed well enough —too well, in fact—but oh, Cypress pitied her. They never let the princess run or ride, or even walk in the sun. The girl had grown plump and soft and so very pale. No one spent time with her except her nurse, a pinched and wizened creature with a voice like a harpy. Cypress only saw the princess at the occasional feast or holy-day, or when visitors came and even the lowest kitchen wenches had to serve in the hall. Rosabella often smiled but never laughed, and her eyes, the scullery maid observed, were always sad. Once, when Cypress had to fetch water from the well, she saw the girl staring out in wonder as snow fell on the ice-silvered rose-canes, their thorns sharp as a wolf's fangs. The gaunt arm of the nurse yanked the princess back inside.

For many years the king and queen had longed for a daughter. They had six fine sons—if by fine one meant richly dressed and sneering. But only the eldest could inherit the tiny kingdom—a ramshackle village and few paltry fields surrounding the castle—and it was costly to find dowries or commissions for the rest. They needed a daughter to sell off in marriage to a wealthy suitor in order to keep the realm solvent. And so Rosabella was swathed in precious silks, bathed in almond milk and crushed flower petals, and stowed away in the rose-choked tower until she could prove her worth.

Cypress worked hard at her lowly chores. In her few spare hours, she wandered in the forest, bringing back to Myllem fresh herbs and hidden gems like chanterelles or wild strawberries. Her gifts added fresh flavors to the meals, so the cook no longer beat her. Cypress brewed tasty tisanes which granted the drinkers restful sleep and sweet dreams. Soon all the servants clamored for them, and even the king and queen called for cups before retiring. The foreigner won new respect, and Myllem no longer thought it beneath her to chat with the girl. Cypress made the kitchen garden flourish, and aided the gardeners with the rose beds and in cutting back the thick canes that threatened to overwhelm Rosabella's tower.

One spring day while Cypress was doing just that, she spoke to the princess. The nurse was away. Now that the princess was almost a grown woman, she often left Rosabella alone for hours at a time, certain she would spend her time suitably; docility had been the primary trait cultivated in her. While Cypress hacked at the canes, her sleeves ripped by the thorns, her arms bleeding, the princess peeked out from the threshold.

Cypress paused in her work. "Wouldn't you like to step outside? It's a fine day."

"I'm not allowed," the princess said meekly.

"Nurse Krimps told me she'd be gone for a few hours."

The girl glanced to her right and left and didn't budge. But she held a hand over her heart and her face was filled with yearning.

"I'll stay by you and protect you," Cypress said, pulling herself up to her full height. She'd grown accustomed to stooping, lest the castle folk feel threatened.

"Would you—could you—take me to the garden?" the princess asked. "I've never seen it."

If Cypress worried about the risk of such an undertaking, the girl's joyful smile made her sorrier she'd never tried before. She held out her arm like a courtier for Rosabella to lean on.

"You go too fast!" the princess complained. "A lady must never take long strides like a man, but show herself to be dainty and fragile." Cypress bit back the desire to argue that the girl was fragile enough. Instead, she shortened her stride and slowed down.

They stepped through the arbor. The garden wasn't much to look at yet; most of the flowers were just green spears poking up from the soil. But the girls bent down to examine each sprout and bud, the patterns of veins on the different leaves, happily comparing all the different varieties of green.

"What do you do all day in that tower?" Cypress asked.

"I learn deportment. How to speak with a soft, silken voice, to say little and listen much. How to smile sweetly but not too broadly. And I embroider. I've embroidered tablecloths and sheets for my trousseau, and thousands of pillow-slips, and ever so many slippers for my ladies in waiting, though I don't have any. Nurse Krimps herself has twenty pairs. My parents send others off to far lands, in the hopes that princes and kings will admire my work and ask for my hand in marriage. I'm rather tired of embroidery, but it does keep me occupied."

"Don't you do anything useful? Sew your own gowns, or card or spin?"

"Princesses aren't supposed to be useful," Rosabella answered, "only beautiful. And of course fetch a good bride price and bear her husband healthy heirs."

"Do you never read? Or sing?"

"Heavens no!" the girl cried. "If I read, my future husband would think me too independent, filled with radical ideas. If he wishes me to know things, he will teach me them himself. As for singing—Nurse Krimps is tone deaf, so she's never taught me any songs. I wish I knew some."

Cypress felt very sorry for the girl indeed, and before she returned her to the tower, vowed that she would visit as often as possible, and help her see a little something of the outside world whenever the nurse was absent.

She was as good as her word. Almost every day, the scullery maid escorted the princess to the garden. Cypress told the Rosabella of her homeland, and taught her many of the island songs. The princess had a lovely voice, faint at first, but gaining in strength over time. Her cheeks no longer resembled the white roses of her tower but the pink ones that now blossomed in the summer garden. She walked briskly, and could even run. She easily learned the names of plants and flowers, and soon her nimble fingers were adept at snapping off dead leaves and spent blooms. She had a quick mind, after all, and had only been trained to be dull. She reminded Cypress of the topiaries that edged the garden walk, twisted out of their true form. But a topiary left unpruned would soon revert to its natural state. Cypress hoped that her friend was now experiencing such a restoration.

One day, when Nurse Krimps was out for most of the day, Cypress brought Rosabella to the woods. She'd told Myllem she would bring back mushrooms and watercress, so she'd been granted three full hours between breakfast and dinner.

"I've never seen so many trees!" the princess exclaimed. "And the light!" She placed her hand in a golden shaft that threaded its way between the trees. Tears starred her cheeks like dewdrops in the morning grass.

That was when Cypress knew she loved her, not merely as a friend, but with a deep, abiding love.

The princess caressed the long needles of a pine. When her fingers came away sticky with sap, she sniffed them. "Will you teach me?" she asked.

"Teach you what?"

"How to hear them. The trees. You said they communicate with you."

"I don't know if they'll speak to your kind," Cypress said. "Besides, it takes years to learn to hear the trees' speech.

"Please, let us try!" the princess begged.

"First you must take off your shoes." Before Rosabella could comply, Cypress bent and removed them herself. The delicate green satin had gotten muddied from their woodland trek, the silk embroidery torn. "Oh, they're ruined! Nurse Krimps will discover our secret and never leave you alone again!"

Rosabella laughed. "I have thousands of slippers. I'll discard these and replace them with another pair; she'll never know. The greenspeech," she insisted.

"Stand with your bare feet on the roots," Cypress instructed. "Wrap your arms around the trunk, your cheek and ear pressed to it. Let it feel and hear your heartbeat, get to know you a little and then listen. Listen hard."

Rosabella did as she was told, her eyes closed, her mouth slightly open. Cypress knew the moment when the princess heard the oak: her eyes flew open and her mouth widened. Her arms tightened around the trunk, her feet pressing deeper against the roots.

When her arms grew slack, Cypress asked, "What did you hear?"

"A song! A song, at first, of sun and the rich taste of soil, and the tickling of ants on bark. And then it spoke to me. It said, *Be brave.* And told me my true, my secret name."

Cypress wondered that the tree would speak so readily to a girl untrained in greenspeech, but then her princess was like none other, and who could hold back their heart from her? "What is it?" she asked, in a hushed voice.

The princess laughed. "Rose. That's hardly a secret name, is it? It's mostly just my real name."

But Cypress knew that trees never err or cheat. The girl was Rose, and though now she most resembled the long-stemmed cultivars of the garden's seemly rows, in her heart of hearts she was like the eglantine that gladdens the forest shadows.

She wished she could tell the princess all that. Instead she asked, "Why are the roses that grow around your tower so strange? I've never seen anything like them."

"They were planted generations ago; the tower was old even then. King Rorum married Queen Merash but he loved another. He waited till she bore him three heirs and then plotted to rid himself of her. He called her mad, shut her in the tower with one of her maids, and wed his paramour. The new queen planted the roses herself, saying they were an offering of love to Merash, white in honor of her purity. But she had knowledge of witchcraft, and the roses grew more quickly than was natural. The thickest hedge was placed before the tower door, the canes climbing and entwining so Merash could never get out."

"So the hedge was built to be her prison," Cypress said.

Rose nodded. "When they put me in the tower, they had to hack away the briers, and remove the bones."

Cypress shuddered. Rose took her hand. "It was long ago. The hedge no longer bars my door."

"You're still a prisoner there."

"I will always be a prisoner." The princess looked up into the boughs of the oak as if she wished she could trade places with it. "When I marry, I'll no longer have this. Or you. Though maybe my husband will be kind to me. Maybe we'll even love each other."

The oak groaned, although there was no wind. *They will choose as her bridegroom old King Mindor, rich and cruel,* it told Cypress. She was glad Rose could no longer hear its voice. *He will not love her. She will exchange one prison for a worse one.*

The castle bustled with activity. The princess would soon reach her majority, and the king and queen were planning a ball — ostensibly to celebrate it, but really to provide her many suitors a last glimpse of her beauty before they offered their bids for her hand. Only Cypress knew the man who'd be accepted. As she scrubbed cauldrons clean, or pruned the tower's rose-canes, she tried to hatch a plan to help Rosabella to escape—if that were what she wished. Surely that was why Cypress' fate had sent her there.

Rose no longer needed to stand on the trees' roots with her bare feet, or even touch them, to hear them. One day when they were in the forest, Rose listened to her oak, the first that had spoken to her. She cried out, tears coursing down her cheeks. And then she laughed loudly, head thrown back.

Cypress wanted to ask what she'd learned but what the trees say to a person is private, only to be shared if the hearer wishes, and Rose didn't offer. *Perhaps,* she thought, *it tells her about my plan to rescue her. Did she weep at the thought of her marriage being prevented? And laugh that my plan would fail?*

"This wedding—it's something you long for?" she asked Rose instead.

"I—no. I have no wish to wed a stranger. If I marry, I would have it be for love and not for gold. I fear finding myself in a worse prison than the one I've lived in all my life. At least here, there is friendship." She smiled at Cypress.

"What if a way could be found to free you—would you take it?"

"And do what? Go where?" The light dimmed from Rose's eyes.

"Wherever you like. I'll take you anywhere you wish to go."

"Like in a tale!" Rose sighed. "It can never be."

"No tale," Cypress said, "though tales will go in the making of my plan. Do you want to hear?"

It took nothing for Cypress to add some extra herbs to her tisanes.

"Nurse Krimps has told me of the princess' curse. How terrible!" she said to Myllem.

"Curse? I never heared o' no curse," the cook replied.

"Why surely you must have been there yourself. Three hedge-witches were invited to her christening but a fourth forgotten. She laid a curse on the infant, saying that she'd prick her finger on a spindle and die on her eighteenth birthday. But one of the other hedge-witches softened the curse, so that instead she'd sleep for a hundred years."

"A hundred years," Myllem went on, as if she'd been the one telling the story in the first place. The tisanes ensured that Cypress' tale was believed and remembered as fact. "I heared the witch meself. That's why they never let the girl spin; embroidery needles is all they let her get at. But prophecies has ways o' makin' themselves happen, mark my word. And woe if the princess' birthday en't soon upon us! A sad thing for Princess Rosabella but worse for the rest of us if the kingdom loses the money her bride price would provide. What's to become of me, I ask you, if the princess sleeps a hundred years, and the castle goes to wrack and ruin?"

"Good thing the spell may break if the right suitor wins his way to the tower," Cypress said.

"Aye, we must pin our hopes on a hero, that's for certain."

"But how will any man get through those hedges?" Cypress continued. "Soon after her sleeping body is discovered, the roses will grow around her, and the thorns turn into spikes."

"Ready to pierce the heroes like pigs on my spit," the cook continued. "I never liked them hedges, but I suppose that's cause I always knew they was cursed.

They'll keep out anyone but the right man. And what if he don't come?"

And so the story circulated. All feared for the day when the princess would turn eighteen. While the suitors gathered thick as flies, Cypress and the princess gathered white roses from the tower's hedge. The night before the ball, Cypress stole into the tower. She tiptoed past the room where Nurse Krimps slept to the chamber where the princess waited, candles lit. They strewed the rose petals onto the bed, pouring beeswax from the burning candles onto them. With the wax still hot and pliable, Cypress molded the mixture into the shape of the princess, eyes closed as if in sleep. Soon the effigy no longer looked like a mere doll but so exactly like the princess that Rose glanced at her looking-glass to make certain she still wore her own face. Its waxen skin looked and felt like real flesh, and its breast rose and fell as if it breathed. Cypress placed a spindle by the wax figure's outstretched hand.

They stole from the tower, taking anything useful for a long journey, including several jewels to trade for horses and lodging. As they passed the tower's threshold, the rose-hedge spoke in greenspeech for the first time. *I will give your tale the ring of truth,* it promised, *and grow thorns sharp as swords, hungry to slice into human flesh and drink human blood.*

The next morning, Nurse Krimps discovered the body of the princess, and the vile spindle, and the kingdom mourned—at least for a time. The hedge rose up, true to its vow, stronger than any wall, brandishing foot-long thorns sharper than swords. But although Rosabella could not be married off to King Mindor or any other suitor, the realm flourished, for the king and queen charged a handsome fee to each man who attempted to broach the hedge. Several inns were built at the foot of the tower to house the would-be heroes, which added significant revenues to the local economy. For generations the little kingdom prospered from the heroes' blood—until one day, they say, a man won his way to the tower, kissed the sleeping form, and it crumbled into dust. The hedge receded, the spines retracting, till it looked no more vicious than any ordinary rosebush.

One night, in a forest a day's ride from the coast, Cypress and Rose dismounted. Cypress built a fire and cooked the last of the food she'd stolen from Myllem's kitchen. The next night they would spend in an inn before buying passage on a ship to the former scullery maid's homeland. They ate in silence.

Rose got up to pat the horses, whispering loving words to them, while Cypress warmed her hands at the fire and gathered her courage.

"That first day the oak spoke to you, why did you cry and then laugh? Is it something you can tell me now?"

Rose left the horses and stepped closer, standing behind Cypress. "At first I cried," she said, "because the oak told me your secret. I hadn't known you loved me."

Cypress exhaled slowly, the fog of her cold breath flying up to the stars. Rose kneeled behind her.

"Then it told me that I loved you. And I laughed because I knew that already." She wrapped her arms around Cypress and laid her cheek against her back, as if she were a tree.

About the story

I envisioned this as a feminist re-telling of a certain familiar fairy tale, but I didn't want that to be apparent early on. The hero's name that came to me was Cyprus, who was a boy. Then I changed it to Cypress, and the tree and plant imagery came to me. That sounded like a girl's name, so I swerved the story into a different direction again--and liked it much better that way.

A question for the author

Q: What's a genre you'd like to write but don't or can't?

A: Interesting question--if I want to do it, I certainly try. I am attempting to write a fantasy novel for children--it's complete, it's even second and third drafted, but it's not ready for prime time yet and I am having to leave it on the back burner for a while till I can grapple with how I do and don't want to change it. I've started a YA novel, about 3/4 through the first draft, and am having trouble with that. And I have many many ideas for other books. So—I am struggling to become a novelist.

About the author

Sandi Leibowitz is a teacher, classical singer, and writer of speculative fiction and poetry. Her works appear in *Mythic Delirium, Liminality,* Ellen Datlow's *Best Horror of the Year 5, Devilfish, Not One of Us,* and elsewhere. She has been nominated for the Rhysling, Pushcart Prize, and Best of the Net awards, and won second- and third-place Dwarf Stars. The author of *The Bone-Joiner,* a collection of poems, she lives in New York.

www.sandileibowitz.com

Koehl's Quality Impressions

Tim McDaniel

Early Wednesday morning, not much past 10:30, I wheezed my way through downtown in my old '31 Ford. Down to White Center, where the city sprawl collided with the suburban rents, resulting in rows of dingy cheap apartment buildings, absentee landlords and the retreats of the old or underemployed. I found the place easily. A building of wooden clapboard, still advertising 'covered parking' even though those parking spaces were filled with rusting Chevys, discarded washing machines, and mildewed mattresses.

I parked along the street and walked up to the front door, then leaned on the button next to the peeling paper with 'Linaman, Manager' penciled on it.

After a long while there was a muffled voice.

"Yeah?"

"Mr. Linaman?"

"Naw, he left months ago."

"You the manager now?"

"Yeah. You a cop or what? No one here been making any calls."

"Nothing like that. I have a small business proposal that you might be interested in."

"A business proposition, huh? So there's money involved?"

"There's money involved." I'd met plenty of guys like him in prison.

"Well come on up, then, I guess. 203."

The door opened, and I climbed the stairs. The thin carpet, perhaps originally a beige sort of color, was held together by stains, and the narrow staircase exuded the tang of cat piss.

Mr. Manager was, as I would have guessed, dressed in an old t-shirt and a pair of sweatpants, and smelled a lot like the staircase. I explained my needs, he articulated his, and we reached an agreement.

I checked out the deceased woman's room next. It was tiny, and the windows didn't open. There were a few sticks of shabby furniture, and one yellowing photograph on a wall, of a young man in a uniform standing in a desert somewhere. The room at least smelled a little better; a lavender-kind of scent lingered there. I closed the door behind me when I left to go back downstairs.

I left the building and took a deep breath. At least the apartment was still vacant. I wouldn't have to make any more deals on behalf of my client. Vampires, we called them, but not the blood-sucking kind. I made a commission on each deal, but they still made me feel like I needed to shower.

"Koehl's Quality Impressions" was stenciled in black gothic letters on the glass of my office door. A little crooked. All it needed was a cheesy little "While U Wait" card taped under it. Well, in this building, this neighborhood, I couldn't expect the clients I used to get at First

Impressions; over there, Pichrenn's name still brought in the classy set, even this long after his death.

Was "Quality" accurate? Well, it's not bragging to say that I can raise ghosts with the best of them. I can make latent ghosts visible, clear as day, short-term or long. At least I can when I can afford to lay my hands on quality equipment. The gear I use now is so shoddy I'm lucky if Fred and Mary can even recognize dear jowly Aunt Greta.

So, yeah, clients were not lined up outside my door. I came in every day, though, in at nine or maybe ten or eleven and out at five or maybe four, when I wasn't out on a job. I couldn't afford to miss any walk-ins. I got the occasional referral of a double-booked or cheap client from my old friend Nol at First Imp, and some job orders from a few regulars, vampires, some of whom I knew from my prison days. But walk-ins, impulse buyers, were my main source of income. Sometimes people do act on whims. I stayed in the office daily, watching TV or reading or surfing for obits or drinking until I could justify the return to my apartment.

The glass on the door was at least frosted. A classy touch. Most of my clients didn't particularly want to be seen from the street, no more than I wanted passersby to see my empty reception room.

Empty it was, when I got back from arranging the vampire feeding. I hung my jacket on the rack near the door.

Ah. There was a new message for me on my computer. I went to the desk and jabbed the button.

"Hello, Koehl." I was sitting in the chair, and I didn't remember sitting down. Lindsay. "I have a job I'd like to discuss with you. I can come by tomorrow about eleven, if that's good for you."

I hadn't seen her since... when? Oh, yeah. Not since the trial.

God, how I wanted to see her again. And I also really wished that, tomorrow at eleven or so, I could be somewhere else, far away.

"I need you to come see me." Pichrenn's voice on the phone had been thin and uneven, air forced through rusty valves. I was in the middle of a job, taking the impression of a young couple's son, four years old at the time of death, but this was Pichrenn, so I called Nolan to take over for me.

This kind of thing wasn't unusual. The job I was doing was routine, though never tell a family that, and Pichrenn often called me away from those to attend him on more interesting cases. Or more high-profile. I figured, and hoped, he was grooming me to take over once he passed on.

I apologized to the couple, saying I had a family emergency, and took a cab over to the address Pichrenn had given me. I found him in one of those huge, lavish condos on 12th, squatting in the corner of a bedroom. The equipment was still boxed, lying in its contoured foam.

The room was dominated by an immense bed, brass. A window took up most of one wall, affording an impressive view of the city and the mountain, and ostentatious abstract paintings garnished the other walls.

There was another bit of apparent abstract art on the peach carpet, a dark red Rorshach image, all that physically remained of the room's former occupant: a bloodstain like an obscene starfish that had been crushed into the floor. There were additional random splashes and splatters on the mussed bed, and even on one of the walls.

Well, this family wasn't shy about displaying their money, if they could afford to keep the condo, untenanted (so to speak), for four and a half months after the murder of the husband. No wonder they could afford Pichrenn himself.

He stood up and looked down at the carpet stain, back straight, perfectly still, but his hands, jammed deep into his jacket pockets, were twisting and pinching the material. He did that a lot, as if his hands were the only vents for whatever emotions roiled within.

Lindsay was next to him, sitting on a clean part of the bed, composed and quiet. Her eyes were on Pichnrenn, but she was breathing a little too heavily.

"The Dudanna murder," Pichrenn said. I raised my eyebrows. The story had been a big one.

"The wife was the one who did it," Pichrenn said. "Made it look like a robbery, or tried to."

"Yeah," I said. "I saw it on TV. Hi, Lindsay."

She nodded at me, her eyes flashing secrets over Pichrenn's lowered bald head.

I said, "Our client, then, must be the dear departed's murderer's sister, is that right?"

Pichrenn smiled. "Right. The sister of the killer. That's what makes it interesting, isn't it?"

I squatted on the floor next to him and surveyed the scene. He was waiting, I knew, for me to see it. Our job, if we did it well enough, would be both a reflection on the murder, and a comment on the client. And of course we had to please our client while doing so, which sometimes meant hiding or disguising our own comments. We were portrait artists. Well, that's how we thought of ourselves. We wanted to do more than get a snapshot of a corpse. Our equipment amplified the energies embedded in the walls, the floor, the air, to reveal not a carcass, but the shade of a living man.

"Not a happy family, I take it," I said. "I mean between the sisters."

"I'd guess not."

"The wife got away with a slap on the wrist, as I recall. The best justice money could buy."

Pichrenn said nothing.

"Sis is, of course, married herself. An older gent, if I recall."

"Very happily married. There've been no reports of trouble."

"Right. And so there would be no jealousy of the sister who snagged the young movie-star-handsome millionaire, no sexual tension at family get-togethers, no younger-sister resentments or buried bitternesses."

"These people were the top predators of the social jungle, Scott. We're not talking about trailer trash."

"Course not."

"Would it make a difference if they were trailer trash? People all do the same things to each other, no matter their positions," Lindsay said. "Cheat on each other, sneak around."

I decided to ask Lindsay what she had meant the next time I was alone with her. But I knew I wouldn't. Betrayal was not something I wanted to discuss. And anyway, Lindsay had a way of making me forget scruples, even as they clearly gnawed at her.

But I had to say something. Something safe. "Sure it would," I said. "They couldn't afford us. They'd have to make peace with their dead and move on."

We were all silent for a time, then I stood up and squatted down again next to the box of highlighters. I took the first one out and stood up, looking the room over again. Then I crossed the room to the bedroom door and extended the tripod. After setting it in place, I put another highlighter just behind and to the left of where Pichrenn still stood. He observed my choices.

I pulled a third highlighter out of the box and placed it just in front of the window. I punched in some settings. Then I looked down at Pichrenn. He cocked his head.

"There was a lot of emotion flying around here, before and during," I said. "The whole area is bound to be saturated."

"Then we wouldn't need three highlighters," Pichrenn said. "I can almost see the remnants without the use of even one."

"You're sensitive, so you don't count. I've set up these two —" I pointed at the one near the door and the one near Pichrenn — "with complementary frequencies. They'll nearly cancel each other out, with just enough bleed-through to give us something to work with. As you say, it's so thick in here that even that amount should be plenty."

"Ummm."

"And the third one, near the window, I've set much lower."

"To pick up the background."

"Right," I said. "With only one, and with all the other energies flying around, all it'll probably pick up will be ghostly half-images, like something seen out of the corner of your eye."

"You did that at the Joshi place," Pichrenn said.

"Are you accusing me of repeating myself? But these will probably be a little weaker, more ghostly. I've been thinking about getting the chance to try this since the Caceres job. There, the energies were so weak there that half-images were the best I could get, but I did think the effect was an interesting one."

Pichrenn nodded. "And why here?" he asked. "A neat effect is just so much dazzle without a purpose to it."

"The energies released during the act," I said, "will be powerful, and I'm sure they'll be compelling as all hell. But they're all of violence, and terror, or its aftermath. We're sure to get some striking images. But what interests me just as much is the underlying tension. I doubt the victim was entirely shocked by his wife's deed."

I chanced a glance at Pichrenn, but his gaze remained focused on the floor, his brow creased. I would have given a pinkie to know his thoughts just then, to know why he wanted me there. Just for the job? Or was he sending me another message? "He knew, he must have known," I said, "that she was on the edge. He probably enjoyed baiting her, flirting with the sister, making her feel unwanted, bullying her, whatever. I don't know. But I'm sure there was something there. If we can display some of that, even as — or especially as — ghostly after-images behind the main action, I think it'll be something worth looking at."

"Hmmm," he said. Lindsay was nodding along.

"And I was thinking. They specified suppression of sounds, knocks, smells, temperature variations, I suppose?"

Pichrenn nodded.

"I don't know if it's totally ethical, but if we allowed a little of the subsonics to leak through..."

"Yes," said Lindsay. She looked over at me.

"Unsettling." Pichrenn got up, bones creaking, and shook a leg that had apparently gone numb. "Very interesting, Scott," he said. "You have a good grasp of things. I believe I'll leave this one in your hands."

I kept my face blank. There was no way he could have found out about what Lindsay and I had been up to. He had called to say he'd be late for a meeting up at his cabin, and things had just happened. And then they happened again, in other places at other times.

"The client paid for your personal attention," I said. "She's bound to be upset."

"I'll smooth things over with her," he said. "If she wants to pay for my judgment, she'll have to accept my judgment that you're the best one for this job."

Maybe that was all there was to it — that he thought I was best for the job.

It kind of makes me sorry that I killed the old guy.

Lindsay settled into the chair and leveled her eyes at me. Lindsay Ingham, Charles

Pichrenn's former lover, or at least the final one. And mine. She used to breeze through the outer offices on her way to his inner sanctum, slim, elegant, and moneyed, with glossy black hair that bounced off the small of her back.

After Pichrenn's death, she'd pretty much disappeared. At the funeral it seemed to me, at least, that an understanding look had passed between us, an acknowledgement that I was still part of her world. But I had been out on a job when she came by the studio to pick up her mementos. She called me twice. I put off answering. But when she heard that I had taken Pichrenn's impression, she vanished. Felt like I'd betrayed him even unto death. Or maybe it was just guilt that she felt, however unwarranted. Our affair hadn't killed him.

Then the law finally caught up with me, and I saw her in the witness box at the trial, and there was prison. She didn't visit.

And now here she was, in my own little studio, in one of those new skirts that's tight in some places and loose in others, and a black blouse with ruffles around her neck. The air was low in oxygen just then, and my gaze stole back to her face, tracing the line of the chin, her cheeks and eyes and hair, whenever she looked down.

"So. Welcome to Koehl's Quality Impressions," I said. "It's uh, good to see you again, Lindsay."

Lindsay looked around her at the decor — the faded carpet, the Degas print on the wall. "Nice," she said. She didn't say it was nice to see *me* again.

"Yeah," I said. "High class all the way."

"Do you keep your equipment here?" she asked.

"I got a closet. This place came with every convenience. So, what have you been up to?"

"I remember you used to only use the best. You know, Charles really admired your ability to keep all of it in such top shape."

So she didn't want to get personal. No old friends and lovers catching up crap. "That's the trouble with the best stuff," I said. "It's temperamental." Like people. I waited for her to talk.

"Charles used to say you were the best in the studio," she finally said, not looking at me. "No knocks, no temperature swings or stopped clocks when you did a job."

The second mention of Pichrenn. "I miss him too, you know," I said, opening and closing a desk drawer for no reason. "I was there with him from the beginning."

"I know. Until the end. Well, if you miss him so much, stop by his place. You can see him anytime there, right?" Her voice had shifted out of neutral, but not in a direction I liked. "Sorry," she said. "I know you didn't mean... I mean, that you never wanted..."

"Don't worry about it. I'm past that. So what's up, Lindsay?" I leaned back in my chair. It creaked a little. I thought Lindsay had perhaps changed her perfume, but I couldn't be sure.

"I need a job done, Scott."

"And you came here? As far as I know they're still taking commissions at First Impressions. They're the best. And I know you always did like the best." I couldn't look too long into her eyes.

"If you're fishing for a compliment, I've given you too many already. Do you want to take the job?"

"I need to hear a little about it first," I said. A lie, but I didn't want her to know how far I'd sunk and how desperate I'd become. Oh, when I first got out on probation, I was the talk of the town, the indispensable impressionist and party guest. Offers both personal and professional came in the daily email. I had turned them all down; they had all been just a different kind of vampire, getting their jollies with a touch of death. But my fifteen minutes had ended.

Back to business. I clasped my hands on my desk. Clients liked it when you seemed to give them your full attention, and going to an impressionist is a little intimidating to some, like going to confession, or revealing your dirty little secrets to a psychiatrist. People take death seriously, even if it's not their own.

"It's my mother."

"I don't remember you talking much about her."

"No. We didn't have a lot of contact the last few years."

"So you had a fight. Teen angst, I suppose?" She didn't say anything. "But now you decide that you want to raise her. Planning to enact a little posthumous make up session, a sort of after- death mother-daughter heart to heart? You know it doesn't work that way." I don't know why I was being such a bastard.

"Look, I just owe it to her. There's nothing else I can do for her."

" 'For her' ? How's that? It's just a damn ghost, Lindsay. It's got as much self-awareness as a black and white photograph. Your mom, she's gone."

"Call it a gesture then. It's too late for anything else." She looked down at the floor, as if the topic were too personal for her to go on. I didn't believe that for a second, but I let it ride. I didn't need to talk myself out of a job.

"OK. You're the customer." I slid a brochure over to her. Nice how desktop printing can make your hole-in-the-wall look like a real-live business. "Here are the rates."

She took it, but she didn't look down at the brochure. At least she didn't crease it; I could use it again next time if she didn't stick it in her purse. "I came to you because you're good. I don't want the effect spoiled by second-rate equipment."

"I don't really have the resources I once did."

"With the advance I'm prepared to pay, you can afford to get some of those resources again." I liked the sound of that; I missed the feel of properly tuned and maintained equipment, its quiet, even hum and ozone smell. The garbage I used now tended to sputter, and the focus kept going out unless you constantly kept on top of it.

Also, an advance that big could pay some of my less important bills, too. Rent and food came to mind.

Lindsay began tapping her code into my paypad.

I forced myself not to look. I pulled up an empty file on the computer, and started filling it out. "I'll need your current address." She took one of her cards out of her purse and passed it to me. I saw that nowadays she was employed at EarthTenders, Inc., a non-profit environmental umbrella. Part-time, no doubt. It was just the kind of feel-good job an over-indulged rich girl would have. It shouldn't have made me so bitter. If she spent her time suckling endangered wildebeest puppies, what was it to me?

"Any other legally interested parties?"

"Mom's latest ex has signed off on it. That satisfies your legal requirements, I believe."

"Sure does." I kept typing. "Visual, audio, olfactory?" Most people want only the visual, even though it's more work to suppress the taps and moans and temperature swings.

"Just the visual."

"Short-term, long-term, or permanent?"

"Short-term."

"OK." I stopped typing and looked at her, but she was doing her stare-at-the-floor act again. I saw a few wrinkles on her face that hadn't been there all those years before.

"I really just have to say goodbye," she said. "I don't need an endlessly repeating exhibition, for people to gawk at." Another little dig at me for raising Pichrenn. So I guess the guilt still gripped her. But I'd show her that nowadays I was immune to that kind of subtle reprimand. I was a businessman now, not some overpaid artiste.

"Short-term it shall be. Cause of death?"

"Her heart."

"OK, good. Place and time of death?"

"June 19th, this year. It was a Saturday. At 9:10 p.m. At 7th and Bell."

I typed. Then, "If the death occurred on the street itself, or in any public area, we'll need all kind of permits."

"That's not a problem. She actually died in a restaurant there, Grasso's. They've already given their permission." She fished some papers out of her purse and passed them across the desk.

Standard release forms. The restaurant probably figured a ghost would be good for business, and maybe they were even right, at least for the short term. But I doubted it. "When can you do it?"

I pulled my appointment book out of a desk drawer and made a show of flipping through its blank pages. "How about this Thursday? Say one o'clock."

"That would be fine."

I didn't suppose the restaurant would object to that hour of the day. The raising of a ghost would be good entertainment for their lunch crowd.

After Lindsay left I sat in my chair, blinking. What the hell had I done? She'd reached out – clumsily, indirectly, but she had made contact. And all my defenses had shot up. I'd needed her, on many levels, after Pichrenn died. My friend, my mentor. According to the law, my victim. And I'd had no one to lean on, because she was dealing with her own issues.

I could still smell her. I didn't know if it was a perfume or just her, but now I knew it hadn't changed from back when. The office was suddenly small, dingy, dark and close. I had to get out.

I had to visit Pichrenn again.

The apartment building was now owned by a foundation that had agreed to allow suite 612 to remain vacant. They rented out the other rooms, and probably not one in ten of the current inhabitants knew that the former occupant up there on the sixth floor had not really left.

The doorman knew.

"Mr. Koehl. Good to see you again." Jacob removed his hat and put it under an arm. I noticed that his hair was graying, the tight curls looking like ash.

"Good to see you, Jacob."

Jacob turned to open the door for me. "Time for the renewal, Mr. Koehl?"

"No. Just a visit."

"Ah." Jacob led the way across the plush lobby to the bank of elevators. "Well, that's important. Remembering." He gently pressed the elevator call button, and the doors opened immediately.

"Yeah, I guess so," I said. We entered the elevator. "Many tourists come by lately, Jacob?"

"Not so many. There was an old lady eight, ten days ago, and some art student early this week."

The elevator car stopped. We paced the cream carpet down to 612. Jacob turned the key in the lock, then stepped back. "Have yourself a good visit, now, Mr. Koehl."

He never came in.

"Thank you, Jacob." I opened the door.

Usually he was in the big easy chair, head up, one hand touching his chin. He must have done that a lot, for it to have imprinted so strongly; he couldn't have planned a better portrait.

And, I must admit, I had done well with the material. Nothing flashy here, nothing avant-garde, not for him. A quiet study of a thoughtful, gentle man. I'd let a sound of even breathing come though. The legs were almost invisible, mere suggestions of lines and the drape of his trousers. But his body became more substantial as you moved up, and the chair back was nearly completely obscured by his torso. The head was preternaturally distinct, the dark eyes burning.

God, I missed him.

The foundation kept some equipment in a closet. I set it up the way I always did, going through the motions, and renewed the imprint. It wasn't time yet, I just needed to do something with my hands. Then I sat in a chair for a while. It doesn't do any good to talk to a ghost. I never know what to say, anyway.

I shouldn't have set the appointment for Thursday. It gave me three days to wait. Sure, I had wanted her to think I was busy, but I could've claimed a sudden cancellation. She'd have seen right through me, but then, she almost certainly already had anyway.

There was one thing I could do. I fed her check to my computer. Now I had the money, I could stop using the shoddy broadcasters that spit all over the spectrum, and the tuneless highlighters and the touchy suppressors. Now it would be topline stuff, paid for in full with Lindsay's advance.

At the shop they greeted me like an old friend who'd killed someone — fair enough. But once we got to going over the equipment — oh, the way those new suppressors squelch noise! — all awkwardnesses and discomforts were forgotten, and I walked out of there with the best stuff I'd ever worked with, and slaps on the back.

Then, of course, I had to go to the scene of death, to scout out the territory. I hoped my car still had some juice in the bat.

It was in a good part of town. A very good part, in fact, where I stuck out like a zombie at a wedding. Grasso's was the kind of place a Mafioso would kill to be murdered in — all indirect lighting, widely-spaced tables, dark reflective wood, candles, and hovering waiters. And expensive. Conscious of my old jacket, my shoe with the loose sole, I didn't want to go in.

I knocked on the glass door anyway.

A guy in a billowy white shirt, his tie undone, peered out at me. I flashed him my business card, which should mean nothing, but flash any sort of ID when you aren't being asked to and people just start thinking police or Homeland Security. He opened the door.

"I'm afraid we're closed," he began.

"Yeah, I figured. Lindsay Ingham asked me to stop by."

"One moment, please." He disappeared into the bowels of the restaurant and soon came back with a Mr. Sarkouhi. Apparently there was no Grasso.

"Ms Ingham mentioned you would come to see the site, Mr. Koehl. Thank you for visiting before we open for dinner." Mr. Sarkouhi, comb-over plastered to his wine-colored skull, a thin moustache drooping against jowly cheeks, nodded me inside. "When you have prepared everything, of course, then we will go public, as they say. The table where it occurred is just through here."

Nothing special about the table. It was against one wall, a painting above it. But I saw some interesting possibilities, and the setting was appealing — death and money, death and elegance; these were and remain powerful combinations. They pushed buttons, and I found myself getting excited by the work ahead. Such a change from that which I had been getting lately.

I made some mental notes. Places I could shoot from, surrounding material resonances. I forgot that Mr. Sarkouhi was hovering behind me until he delicately cleared his throat.

"I'm almost finished, Mr. Sarkouhi. Just figuring the angles."

"Of course, Mr. Koehl. The passing of Ms Mehrer in our establishment was, I'm sure you understand, quite a shock."

"I'm sure it was."

"What I mean is, Ms Mehrer was more than a customer here. She was here so often, and she enjoyed a close relationship to those here, the staff and the other diners."

I could see what he was working up to. "Do you suppose they'll enjoy seeing her here again?"

"It might be disquieting to some."

"And yet Lindsay told me you agreed to the raising. She showed me the paperwork."

"Yes, that's true. It's just that, well…"

"I know. I guess you don't say no to Lindsay." I never could, for different reasons. Or maybe they weren't so different. "Mr. Sarkouhi, she's asked for just a temporary raising. I'll make sure it's as tasteful as I can. I don't know what else I can tell you."

"Thank you, Mr. Koehl. And my thanks, again, for coming when we are closed between lunch and dinner. I appreciate that you are trying to minimize the disruption."

"No problem." Actually, I hadn't even thought about the restaurant being open or not.

As Mr. Sarkouhi turned away, a thought struck me. "Mr. Sarkouhi. On the night in question, was Ms Mehrer dining alone?"

Mr. Sarkouhi's face flushed a deeper red. "Ah, no, Mr. Koehl. She was dining with her husband."

Her husband? Lindsay hadn't shown me any paperwork from him. And I would need it. As she well knew.

Back in the office, I called up the news stories about the death of Ms Mehrer on the computer.

Alicia Mehrer had indeed died of a heart attack on June 19th, at 9:10 p.m., at Grasso's. According to witnesses she murmured something, stood up, took a few steps and then collapsed, dying a few moments later.

I wondered at the last name. I looked up Lindsay's bio. Skimpy. She must have paid someone monstrous sums to keep her bio so short. But it did show that her dad, Joseph Ingham, had left the family when she was just seven. The mom remarried two years later. The second husband had died. Cancer. Then mom had married Joseph again, and divorced him again two years after that. Well. Sounded like an interesting family. Money and death, and Lindsay's family had a lot of both. But with a divorce on record, at least I wouldn't have to meet the old man to get a signature.

My computer search turned up plenty of gossip concerning the late Alicia and her ex Joseph. Curiosity got the better of me and I expanded the search a bit and came up with some charming hospital records. All of the sources agreed that Mr. Ingham had been one real bastard. The kind of guy a jury would wink at you for killing.

And yet, even after the abandonment and after the divorce, Alicia had kept coming back for more pain. Again and again.

Sex and death is another powerful combination; the oldest and the strongest of them all.

And why had Lindsay neglected to mention that her dad was with her mom at the time?

Closet skeletons can make a raising a lot more interesting.

Thursday. The restaurant door opened, and Lindsay entered with the grace of a predatory eel, dressed all in satiny black. She stood and watched me work for a while. Of course, a small crowd had already gathered; the equipment summons them as reliably as it summons ghosts. Mr. Sarkouhi stood prominently in the center, his arms folded in pride, surveying the crowd.

Lindsay came closer. "How's it going?" If she was so cool and commanding, why did her fingers clench her bag?

"Just finishing up the underlays now." I tightened a tripod leg, then checked the broadcast shadow.

"I've decided to go long-term, Scott."

I looked up. "What?"

"I said I've decided to go long-term. With an option for permanency."

I looked at Mr. Sarkouhi. "It's all right," Lindsay said. "Mr. Sarkouhi has given us permission."

"I'll need to see that for myself."

"Of course." She opened her purse without looking at it and took some papers out. She held them out to me.

"Why the change in plan?" I left her holding the papers and picked up another broadcaster.

Lindsay was silent for a short time. "Does it matter?" She allowed her hand to drop to her side, the papers slapping against her tailored slacks.

"No, I guess not." I extended the tripod legs on the broadcaster and set it up at a 45-degree angle to the first. I'd put a highlighter just between the two. "You just wanted to say goodbye — wasn't that the purpose of this raising?"

"Maybe I just thought I would need more time with her." I didn't even pretend to look convinced, and she continued, "She *was* my mother, Scott."

I flipped the test switch on the 'caster and checked the levels as it hummed. "Not a very private place for getting in your quality time with mom." I adjusted the levels and checked the output. I looked up at her.

Lindsay looked at me, her eyes just slightly narrowed. I knew why she had chosen me for the job. Not because I was the best, but because she knew that I would do it, that I would gratefully touch things more reputable studios sneered at.

Or there was another reason, but I veered away from that thought.

"Well, if you change your mind, remember I do collapsings, too," I said. "In fact, I lay more ghosts than women." It was a standard joke, and she gave it the response it deserved.

"Are you ready?"

"Another ten, fifteen minutes."

"Fine." Lindsay passed the papers to Mr. Sarkouhi and greeted some oldsters sitting at a nearby table. Mr. Sarkouhi stood there, one hand on his moustache, not looking at anything.

"I guess you'll be getting a permanent tourist attraction, right here at table eight, Mr. Sarkouhi," I said.

"Permanent, maybe." Sarkouhi looked less than thrilled.

"None of my business, but it seems to me that what might attract a crowd for a short while might grate on the nerves of your diners, if it's constantly in view. Of course, you'd be a better judge than me of what might pique a person's appetite."

Sarkouhi narrowed his eyes. "If you talk me into withdrawing my permission, Mr. Koehl, you'll lose the job."

"Last thing on my mind, Mr. Sarkouhi."

"I could revoke permission, though, at a later date. Couldn't I? I read the contract."

"Yeah, maybe. But Lindsay might try to sue if you try it. The lawyers would have to decide what your contract actually says. Better to just curtain off the table."

Sarkouhi met my eyes briefly, then nodded thoughtfully.

Memories intrude like unwanted ghosts.

The day Pichrenn died, I'd gone to see him at home. That memory was a persistent visitor. He'd been sick for some time, and he'd had his bedroom outfitted with all kinds of medical equipment and monitors. The place smelled of disinfectants and futility, and Pichrenn lay in his huge bed, looking over at me with eyes too bright in a head become too large.

His voice was as weak as his body, but he could still speak, was still coherent.

"Art," he told me. "That's been my life, Scott, these last thirty years."

"And you've done well," I said. "You know how impressions were looked at before you got into the field. Dodgy at best. You made a whole new artform. I guess not many can claim that distinction."

Pichrenn smiled sickly, not falling for the flattery, sincere though it was. "And now this." With an arm little more than papery skin stretched over knobby bones, he gestured at the IV feeds, the machine that beeped his heart along. "They tell me I could live ten more years like this."

What could I say to that?

"They're making advances all the time."

"So maybe I'll only lie here for eight years, or six. That's no way to be, Scott. But the law says I can't take the easy way out, with ten 'good' years ahead of me. Damn Republicans."

I looked away.

"Help me, Scott." He whispered it.

And then, "Make me a work of art."

"Huh?" But I knew.

There is no kind of death that can compare with a properly-conducted suicide. Despair, desperation, pain, a reckless courage, and even a strange sort of hope: that someone will stop you, that you'll be delivered into heaven, whatever. It makes for one hell of an impression.

And it's almost as hard to kevork as it is to do it yourself. Sure, lots of laws make it all right to kill someone, if they really want you to, and if the doctors have signed off on the sign-off. But that's not what Pichrenn was asking for, a sterile room and a certifiably painless fade out. My way would be less clinical.

But afterwards, I made the impression, and it's still drawing the occasional connoisseur. Maybe Pichrenn, or part of him, thought he was doing me a favor, giving me so much pain to work with.

Lindsay came over, ushered by a hostess. "Everything's ready?"

"Yep."

"Fine. Let's do this."

Sarkouhi raised his eyebrows at me. I nodded.

"I think your host would like to get everyone here for the unveiling," I said. "That's his payoff, right? That he can show this off to his customers."

"Who knows why anyone does anything. He gave his permission. That's all I needed."

"Still, we can give him a minute to get his people assembled." I made some final, unnecessary adjustments. "I have to say that I don't feel this will be representative of my best work, Lindsay. The image is fairly clear and sharp, but the background hum is, at best, just…"

"I don't need art. I just want to see Mother."

"Well, then everything's fine."

Sarkouhi, all smiles and broad gestures, led a small group of his well-fed and overdressed patrons into a semicircle around the table. I showed them where they could stand for the best view, then stood before them. I waited for their gossiping to slow to a trickle, their eyes to wander to me.

"Before I unveil this, I'd like to clear up a few common misconceptions about my craft, for those who may not be as deeply involved in the netherworld as I am," I said. I saw that Lindsay was annoyed with my delay, but hell, this was too good a chance to pass up. I just might pick up some high-class clients.

"First, what this is not." I started passing out business cards. "Ghosts are not self-aware, they're not beings. They can't see you or hear you. They're simply impressions, imprinted on the local area by the trauma of death. Or by other trauma, or other emotion. That's why you sometimes see ghosts of the living." I'd passed out all my cards. Time to wrap it up.

"The impressions are often of the moment of death, but not always." I went back to my equipment. "Dominant feelings, commitments left unfulfilled, unsaid messages, all these things can and do show up, and it's up to the artist to see that they do. And that's all I have to say. Let's see what we can see."

I checked my viewer. Yeah, I was satisfied with what I had called forth. I flipped the final switch.

At first there was nothing, except for the low hum of the 'caster. The smell of ozone grew in the air. Slowly an image started to form, in mid-air next to the table. It started as a grainy mist, like fine television snow, a vague human shape. It slowly intensified and clarified as the highlighters brought more of the energy out into visible forms, kicking it to the focusers. All this was needed to get the image formed in the first place — although of course natural ghosts do form, usually of an inferior quality, and with odd, annoying, aural and temperature effects — but once it was there, it would stay until properly laid, as long as it got boosted now and then.

The image continued to clear, and soon we were looking at a woman. It was a loop. Not uncommon. She moved, in jerky, uncertain movements, from the table to a spot a few feet away. Then suddenly we would see her lying on the floor, face down. Then she would be up again, moving around, as if confused. Her death had obviously come as a shock to her.

Her body, her clothes, were not too distinct — vague suggestions of a matronly form, decked out in some kind of conservative dark dress. Maybe the neckline was a bit lower, the dress a bit tighter, than society would choose to dictate. Was that a string of pearls around the fleshy neck? It was hard to tell.

But none of that mattered. Because the face — the face was clear, very clear. Real.

It was an aged face, but not heavily lined; Lindsay's mother would have been happy to hear that her face-lifts had survived her death. The forehead, fringed by curled white hair, was nearly smooth, the cheeks still full, the chin small and weak but still single.

You could see all that eventually. But it took time to take in, because what caught the attention were the ghost's eyes. They were startlingly blue in that papery face, and as the woman paced they sought something, something to be wary of. You could almost see a hunched form, a shadow, a dark aura, hovering at her back. And the expression in Mrs. Mehrer's eyes—

They were imploring. That's the word. But why? Was Ms Alicia Mehrer asking for mercy, for freedom? Or for understanding, compassion? There was shame in those eyes, too.

Even in death, she remained in thrall to her husband, bound to him by pain and need.

I couldn't have manufactured such a thing. But an impressionist can choose what to highlight — lives are complicated things — and I'd made sure that sick dependency came through. Call it art, showing a truth in place of the prettified picture that was asked for. Call it a stab at Lindsay. I don't know.

Maybe it was just what Lindsay had wanted to see. I had to look over at her. Her expression was at first smug, then horrified, lips parted and wide-eyed, but soon a mask slid down over her face. Her eyes narrowed and the right edge of her mouth curved up slightly. She coolly surveyed the onlookers; before her eyes met mine, I quickly looked down.

Then I looked at the crowd. I'd seen the same reactions a hundred times before. Some looked on in horror, lips curled, and clutched at the arms of those next to them. Some tried to avert their eyes, as if embarrassed, but their gazes were continually drawn back to the apparition before them. And some few leaned forward, drinking in the death.

Sarkouhi was watching the crowd, too. He seemed less than pleased. He saw me looking at him and walked over to me.

"Is this normal?" he asked in a low voice. "I mean, will it do anything else?"

"Some few do seem to react to things near them. Some look like they are trying to talk to you — the impressions can react to the impressed energies of those still living. Some act out the worries on their minds at the moment of death. Sometimes they even communicate what that was. Or try to. But, to answer your question, no. This is it. It's a fairly short action loop this time. She wasn't here long enough to lay down much more narrative."

Sarkouhi looked back at the impression, his face sour. I began packing up my stuff. Sarkouhi looked back at me.

"You're leaving?"

"Yep. Job's done."

"And this will just go on, repeating here in my place?"

"That's right." I folded a tripod and laid it gently in its foam-lined case. "I've pumped a lot of energy into the floor and walls, enough to keep it going for at least five or six weeks. And after that, I'll come back and pump it up some more. Can I use your phone? I have to call to have this stuff picked up." I couldn't just toss equipment of this caliber into my trunk, but it was humiliating to have to ask.

"Of course." He handed it over and I turned to the wall to give the man a moment, and sure enough, Sarkouhi went to talk to Lindsay.

Their conversation apparently didn't last too long, because when I clicked off and resumed packing, Sarkouhi was over by the other restaurant patrons. I guess he was trying to put a good face on the show, but the diners weren't buying. Several had already left, and a few in the back were realizing that they would have to pass uncomfortably close to the ghost to get to the door.

"Mrs. Sorensen!" Lindsay called, and one of the biddies looked up. A much younger man, his hair still dark, put a protective arm on her shoulder.

Lindsay made no attempt to get closer to her. "Enjoying the show, Mrs. Sorensen?"

"It's, ah..."

"Not sure? Perhaps your latest young man has an opinion — what's this one's name?"

The man scowled, whispered something to Mrs. Sorensen, and they turned away. Then she pulled away from him and looked back.

"I didn't know, Lindsay. I swear, I didn't know what he was doing to her." She turned and walked away.

Lindsay looked after them, her mouth fixed in its smile, her eyes full of hate.

Then she blinked and looked back at her mother for a moment. She strolled over to me. "Good work, as always."

"Thanks. And the rest of the money will be in my account when, exactly?"

"Oh, how you've come down in the world, Scott." She fished around in her purse and then started writing out a check.

"Yep. All the way down to the bottom line." I swiped her check through my reader. "Pleasure doing business. Please remember me whenever a loved one dies on you." I went back to the packing.

"This is my mother, Scott. You make me sound like one of your ghouls."

I folded a tripod and lay it gently in its foam. "The term is 'vampire.' But you're right. I know that you had me do this out of the love and respect you hold for your dear mom."

Lindsay moved in front of me, and spat her words. "You, of all people, have no right to judge me. I paid you for the job, and you did it. You didn't complain."

"I'm no judge, Lindsay." I closed and locked the lid on the case. I stood up. "They are, though." I nodded over to the last of the restaurant patrons. "You've given them a good show." I couldn't resist. "Was it the one you wanted?" I really was curious about that.

"You're done here, I think," she said, and walked out of the restaurant, almost striding through her mother's image.

Lindsay, Lindsay, Lindsay. Our shared betrayal of Pichrenn had eaten away at us both. Maybe my time in prison had given me a chance to let it go just a little more than she had, had convinced me that she was now out of reach, a subject of wistfulness and what-if. And how did she feel, now? No way would she think of me as out of her league; she could scrape me off the sidewalk any time she felt like it. But having me in her life would just remind her of what we had done to Pichrenn, how our relationship had been tainted from the start by that duplicity.

Sarkouhi headed over to me. I was getting downright popular. "This," he said, "is a bad business."

"Disappointed with the show? You're not alone."

"Oh, Mr. Koehl, I'm sure you have done an excellent job. But this is... It's not dignified."

"Death usually isn't."

He looked at me. "This isn't just death. How can I serve food, with this obscene thing here?"

Dear, dead Ms Mehrer continued her routine.

He hadn't thought of that before? Just what kind of idiot was he? Or, more to the point, what had Lindsay done or said to him? "You'd be surprised," I said. "This kind of show does bring a certain subset of the population. Not like your current crowd, though." I waved a hand at the people. "Like I said, you can always withdraw permission, Mr. Sarkouhi. These things are a lot easier to collapse than they are to bring out. And I work for reasonable rates."

"Ah. Mr. Koehl. As you reminded me, Lindsay Ingham has very many friends."

"She can make trouble for you, is that it? Not just legally."

"That is it."

"Looks like she's making trouble for you, anyway, Mr. Sarkouhi."

"That she is, Mr. Koehl."

As I climbed into my car I saw Lindsay watching the ghost through the window of the doorway, smoking an actual cigarette, the smoke making her features a little unclear. You can't do that in a restaurant. It's slow suicide. That wouldn't bother anyone, but even worse, it's public suicide.

The next day I was sitting in my office, staring out the window. I felt like shit. With the money and new stuff, paid bills, I should have felt like a pop star. Instead I kept seeing Ms Mehrer's face, and I felt like a whore.

The phone buzzed. I picked it up, and there was my vampire, Justin Hoben — excuse me, "John Robertson". The idiot called himself that, and then paid me through his personal account.

"John."

"You said to call today. You said that you would scout out the, that job we talked about."

"Yeah, John."

There was a pause. "Well?"

I didn't know why I was giving him a hard time. Lindsay's money would only last so long, and the bills would come due again eventually. So I roused myself. "Yeah, John. I checked it out. The manager is willing to go along, except he wants a cut. The usual amount, three hundred, and there's my fifty negotiating fee, on top of the baseline costs."

"Yeah, that's fine. When?"

I made a show of looking at my watch, although he wouldn't see it. "I guess I could squeeze it in late this afternoon, say four o'clock, if that works for you."

"Yeah, that would be good for me. Four o'clock."

I hung up. Sure, Mr. Hoben, that time works for you. I figured it would. Your wife thinks you're still at work, your office thinks you've left for the day. That works for you just fine.

It was sacrilege to use the new equipment for a job like this. Wiping grandma's priceless china with a rag made of old underwear. I could just as easily dig out my old stuff. My Mr. Robertson deserved no better.

But the lure of using that fine new gear was just too strong. My breath actually quickened as I thought about it. I felt like a pervert at a schoolyard. But I got it out anyway, and by three I was on my way.

Once there, it didn't take long for me to set up. Everything snapped into place just as it ought to, just as it used to. No sputtering, no loss of definition or control or focus, no stray signals. I played with the fine tuning, bringing out effects and details I hadn't been able to play with in years.

The old woman had died in the chair, just slumping further down, further down. No drama, just death. Her image flickered at the edges a bit; I toned it down, then brought it back up just to the edge of sight. She kept her eyes half closed, and she seemed to be mindlessly staring at something, probably a television set that the landlord sold off when the body was found. She wore a gray blouse, and a necklace of fat glass beads, red and brown. She also wore some fading blue jeans. She was barefoot.

Some current celebrities say in their wills that their houses or places of death should be destroyed, to forestall this kind of thing from ever happening to them. The rest of us can't afford that kind of protection, though there are restraint policies that are supposed to prevent the kind of thing I was doing. The very poor, though, are wide open to the predations of vampires after death.

My vampire knocked at the door. I opened it. "John."

"Mr. Koehl." Justin Hoben's eyes barely brushed me before they focused on the dying woman. His breath caught in his throat.

"I'll be outside." I went down the stairs and I heard Justin close the door and lock it.

I sat in the open door of my car. It's a shame I never took up smoking; it would pass the time. I watched the traffic go by, the single occupants of single vehicles. An hour or so later Justin came back out. His shirt was no longer tucked into his pants, and there was drying sweat on his flushed face. He walked up to me, and didn't look at me as he slipped me his check.

But after he turned away, he spoke.

"You're a genius," he said, his voice thick with emotion. "That was the best — the best I've ever had. Amazing." Still without looking at me, he said, "Thank you," then hurried away.

So the new equipment had an endorsement.

I went back upstairs, and put down the ghost.

Afterwards I drove slowly past Grasso's, though it wasn't on the way home. Grasso's didn't look to have many customers. I laughed, and went home, wishing I had eaten something so I could vomit it back up.

The next morning Lindsay was already in my office corridor when I arrived.

"Where the hell have you been?" she greeted me. She stubbed out her cigarette in her pocket ashtray. "It's almost noon."

"Hello, Miss. Did an appointment slip my mind?"

I unlocked the door and Lindsay followed me inside. She sat down, a firm line to her mouth and a hard look in her eye.

"Have a seat," I said. I seated myself behind my desk and rested my chin on my hands. "Something I can do for you?"

"More like something you did *to* me."

I leaned back. That gaze was a little too intense. "I don't understand, Lindsay. I did what you asked. The ghost hasn't collapsed, has it?"

"To hell with you, Koehl."

"Yep, anyone with one good eye can see the sick relationship she had with your dad. It's all there for everyone to see. And that's exactly what you wanted."

"It's disrespectful, mocking her like that. I wanted a tasteful—"

"In a restaurant. Yeah. Please, Lindsay."

"Go to hell." She folded her arms, looked away, and began to sniff.

"Cut the act, Lindsay. We both know what you wanted. You wanted to leave a bitter taste in the mouths of all her society friends. You hated them for not stepping in, or you hated them for leading perfect lives within calling distance. You hated her for what she allowed your dad to do to her, and you couldn't resist a little public humiliation. And I gave it to you. Just like you knew I would. Because I've got the eye to see it, and the technique to show it, and the desperation to accept the job in spite of all that."

She ended her pretense of crying, and just sat there. I wondered what she wanted, why she was here. To justify herself in my eyes —Oh, I never expected to see *that* — or to gloat with me over her triumph over her mother?

Gloat with *me*? Did Lindsay have no friends?

Did I care? "You always were a little self-centered. Justifiably so. But hardly blind — did you think the relationship obvious to her old friends would slip past me? I do know my work, Lindsay."

"Your work! Raising ghosts for perverts!"

"Don't worry. I don't discuss my clients with anyone."

I should have seen the slap coming. Maybe I did. Then Lindsay stood up and turned her back to me.

The inside of my cheek had been cut by a tooth, and I tasted blood.

"He hated you, you know. Towards the end. That was his parting shot — saddle you with a murder charge."

"Manslaughter." I kept the disinterested tone in my voice, but her words rang in my head. Pichrenn had hated me? I had practically been his son.

And yet — it rang true, also. It didn't come as big a surprise as it should have.

"He taught me well. I owed it all to him. He had no reason to resent me."

Lindsay turned back to me. "Idiot! It wasn't your skill he resented!"

"I never—"

"You didn't need to."

She glared at me, expecting me to — what? Kiss her? Slap her, like Bogart in some old movie? Explain away the thing we'd had behind the old man's back, when I'd been the favored son and it was clear that Lindsay would be free after the old guy had passed on?

I knew that there are ghosts all around us, hovering just at the edges of sight, on the fringes of our minds, as we go about our lives. I made my living revealing them. Now Lindsay was showing me others.

"Why do you keep renewing him, Scott? Why don't you let him fade out?" Her voice was flat.

I had no answer.

"He's gone, Scott. And you blamed me. You never returned my messages."

Had she left messages? I'd told myself for so long that she had cut me loose. But yes, she had left messages I had brushed off. After killing Pichrenn, how could I just go on, take up openly with his lover?

I couldn't think of anything to say, and Lindsay stalked out. Was I supposed to call her back?

Had all this been her way to get through to me?

I've always had trouble with moving on. Maybe everybody does. But I thought a lot about what Lindsay had said, there at the end. I sat in my apartment in the dark, the TV on with the sound turned low, and decided that maybe it was time to act, and maybe even time for Lindsay to take another peek at the sunlit world.

Me too. I not only have trouble moving on, I have trouble going back. Lindsay had reached out to me, coming to see me about a ghost; she had made contact, however awkwardly, and maybe that's the only way she could do it. Still, she had done it. She had tried to show me herself at her most vulnerable, most unappealing, most venal, and most real. I could, too.

I had no idea if she would show up or not. The message I'd left hadn't given her any details, any reason to see me, just the time and place. I watched Pichrenn in his chair, and tried not to think about it. About where she was now, what she was doing, that she was still in the world even though she wasn't in mine.

The door opened. "Scott."

Lindsay stood there.

"Lindsay."

She entered hesitantly. "I'm not sure what I'm doing here."

"Yeah. Neither am I. But I'm here."

She nodded as if that made sense. She crossed the room to the window. She hadn't looked at Pichrenn. She wasn't wearing black this time — light blues and yellows.

I joined her. "I need to tell you something, Lindsay."

She nodded, but didn't say anything.

It was easier talking when she wasn't looking at me. "It's like this. Yes, I killed Pichrenn. He asked me to do it, and maybe he had more than one motive. I don't know. But I know that I've never forgiven myself, for that and for — you know. Us. And afterwards I pushed you away, like it was your fault or something. But I'm tired of pushing."

She turned to me. Her eyes flickered to the impression, then back to me. "You don't have to—"

"Yeah, I do. I really do. Since I got out of prison, since even before that, I've been moping and cynical, and it's got me nowhere. Maybe I've been a little too much in love with death. Maybe that's a job hazard. But I'm tired of it. Finally, I'm just *tired* of it."

I went to the closet and pulled out a single piece of equipment. I didn't even need a tripod. I could just hold it and point it at the apparition.

"Scott — you're..?"

"Time to say goodbye."

I pointed, and pressed the button, and Pichrenn vanished.

Lindsay looked at the chair where the impression had been. I couldn't tell what she was thinking.

I held out the defocuser to Lindsay. She looked at it as if she didn't recognize it, but didn't take it. I put it on the chair.

"If you ever want it, here it is," I said. "It's easy to use. Runs on batteries. Just point, and push the nice red button." I walked to the door. Lindsay still hadn't moved.

At the door I turned. "I usually have dinner weeknights at a little place on Fifth, near Pike," I said. "Rommie's. It's easy to find. I'm usually there from seven-thirty to eight-thirty or so."

I walked out.

Maybe Lindsay was tired of death, too. Tired of looking back.

I'd have to wait and see.

About the story

Ghosts are a fascinating topic. I can't say I believe in them, and yet there is a smudge of doubt; some of the stories are not easy to dismiss. But if ghosts really do exist, what could they be? The idea that they are conscious entities seems nightmarish and unfair to me – can you imagine wandering around an old house for a hundred years, no one to talk to, nothing to read? So the idea came to me that ghosts could be a phenomenon, an imprint of some kind on the structures they inhabit, that science just hasn't unearthed yet. And if that were true, maybe a technology could be developed to make them more easily seen.

Ghost stories are dark stories, generally, so I thought it might be fun to tell a sort-of ghost story using a dark template – that of noir fiction. Instead of a private eye played by Bogart, I would have a guy who uses technology to raise ghosts (but also played by Bogart, if he's available). And then the other elements – a lead character down on his luck, and beautiful woman he has trouble connecting to, a dark past, unsavory acquaintances. And an ending that is not quite completely happy.

A question for the author

Q: Do you live near where you were born? Have you traveled much?

A: I grew up in the Seattle area, went to university in the Seattle area... pretty boring. But after graduation I applied to join the Peace Corps. They decided to send me to South Yemen (this was before South and North united). But, a couple of weeks before I was scheduled to ship out, I got a call telling me that our visas hadn't been approved. Should they look for another assignment? Yes! I'd already sold my car, quit my job!

So a few weeks later I was sent to Thailand. After three months of intensive language and culture training, I was sent to a small village in Pichit province, Kampaengdin ("Dirtwall"). My duties were twofold: to teach English at the junior high school there, and to work with local farmers in some way. Well, I enjoyed the teaching, and did my best to see that the village farmers connected with agricultural officials, and even gave them information about raising fish in their rice paddies.

Normally Peace Corps assignments are for two years, but I applied for, and was granted, a third year, so I could work with various local schools on their English curricula. Then, as I was preparing to go home, I was told of a job offer at a university in the northeastern city of Khon Kaen. I went up there to see if it looked interested, and was immediately offered the job.

I loved it, but after a year came back to the U.S. I'd felt something of an imposter, since I only had a B.A. Back in Seattle I got my Master's in teaching ESL, and then heard that Khon Kaen University wanted me to come back, so I did. Six years later, the Thai economy crashed, so I returned to the U.S.

While living in Thailand I did a little traveling — Myanmar, Cambodia, Laos, Japan, Taiwan, and Nepal.

About the author

Tim McDaniel teaches English as a Second Language at Green River College, not far from Seattle. His short stories, mostly comedic, have appeared in a number of SF/F magazines, including F&SF, Analog, and Asimov's. He lives with his wife, dog, and cat, and his collection of plastic dinosaurs is the envy of all who encounter it. In his spare time (ha!) he teaches judo.

His author page at Amazon.com is www.amazon.com/author/tim-mcdaniel

Copyright

Metaphorosis Publishing

Metaphorosis offers beautifully written science fiction and fantasy. Our projects include:

Metaphorosis Magazine

Metaphorosis, a weekly magazine of SFF short stories, including stories from all the authors in this anthology. Find out more at magazine.metaphorosis.com, and sign up to be notified of new stories.

Metaphorosis Books

Recent books from Metaphorosis can be found at books.metaphorosis.com, and include:

Metaphorosis 2017

Metaphorosis 2016

All the stories from *Metaphorosis* magazine's second year.

Almost all the stories from *Metaphorosis* magazine's first year.

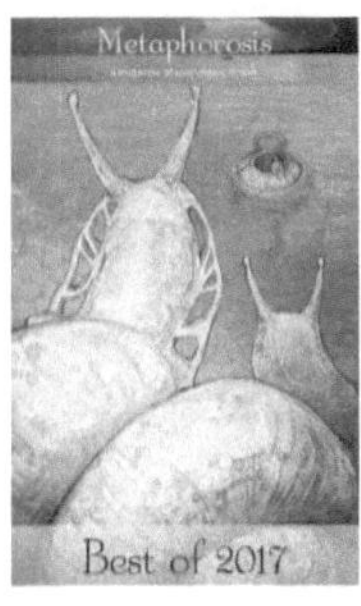 

**Metaphorosis:
Best of 2017**

The best science
fiction and fantasy
stories from
Metaphorosis' 2nd
year.

**Metaphorosis:
Best of 2016**

The best science
fiction and fantasy
stories from
Metaphorosis' 1st
year.

Reading 5X5

Five stories, five times

Twenty-five SFF authors, five base stories, five versions of each – see how different writers take on the same material.

Reading 5X5

Writers' Edition

All the stories from the regular, readers' edition, plus two extra stories, the story seed, and authors' notes.

Best Vegan SFF of 2017

The best vegan science fiction and fantasy stories of 2017!

Best Vegan SFF of 2016

The best vegan science fiction and fantasy stories of 2016!

Susurrus

A darkly romantic story of magic, love, and suffering.